Extinction
Rise Of Mankind Book 8

John Walker

DISCLAIMER

This is a work of fiction. Names, characters, business, places, events, and incidents are either the products of the author's imagination or used in a fictitious manner. Any resemblance to actual persons, living or dead, or actual events is purely coincidental. This story contains explicit language and violence.

Blurb

A Freak Mishap

The Behemoth returns from their latest mission only to find themselves tapped again by the Alliance Intelligence Division. A message was received from an unknown part of the galaxy, filtered through dozens of relays before arriving at the home world. An old friend seems to be stranded and needs assistance yet they were unable to convey proper coordinates.

Meanwhile, The Crystal Font finds itself in the middle of nowhere near an alien world emitting a strange, unknown energy field. Stuck with a broken engine and unsure if help is on the way, they're forced to perform repairs on their own. But as they attempt to rectify their situation, they are attacked by enemy forces.

Racing against time and fighting for survival, The Crystal Font knows they may never make it home but after defying the odds so many times, they refuse to give up. Forced to visit the strange world, they have no idea The Behemoth is looking for them or the bizarre information they may uncover on the idyllic landscape of the planet below.

Prologue

Siva Wih'Faren browsed the incoming traffic from hundreds of intelligence sources across the galaxy. She had operatives stationed in places her government didn't even know they had a foothold in and they transmitted data constantly. Her people even managed to infiltrate the Earth government, which took a little body modification to avoid detection.

Humans had such a limited set of colors for eyes and hair, after all.

Earth people factionalized easily and it concerned Siva's superiors. An entire *anti-alliance* group protested their participation in the galactic theater, pushing that they should remain isolated. Luckily, the government and an overwhelming majority held them at bay but that didn't mean the alliance wasn't going to keep an eye on them.

If at some point those irrational fools ever attained enough power to challenge the authority of the majority, then the kielans may have to intervene. That was one of the jobs her operative was responsible for: ensuring they kept tabs on the various leaders of each group and remained close to them.

A little assassination wouldn't be amiss if absolutely necessary and Siva had plenty of people killed for less. She determined that on her watch, the alliance worlds would remain in check and not cause trouble. Though she wasn't able to focus solely on the war, she fully expected those without her responsibility to do so.

Patriotism meant a lot at such times.

Her people bustled about her, crunching numbers and looking for clues as to threats which might crop up for the alliance. This went beyond the obvious enemy, the one they'd been at war with and extended to internal and external concerns like the Orion's Light terrorists. Such fringe groups were dangerous enough to be a credible threat to security, even if they couldn't necessarily take down the government all on their own.

Each of their chaotic agendas meant they could not be ignored. Siva's team constantly worked to infiltrate these groups, to destabilize their ability to operate and ultimately, break them down completely. However, in some cases, most notably with Orion's Light, it was easier said than done. Some of these groups were particularly rough on recruits.

And few operatives wanted to experience permanent physical alteration for the cause.

Trellan En'Dal volunteered for the hardest task and seemed likely to get the job done with Orion's Light. He'd managed to make contact once and carried something the leadership of that group would desperately want after their last engagement. Luckily, the human vessel Behemoth managed to thwart their overall objective of sowing disorder in an alliance controlled system.

Trellan took advantage of the situation and did his best to prove his worth. If it panned out, he'd be able to get close to their leader and finish them off. All intelligence reports indicated that Krilan Ar'Vax held the group together through sheer will alone. In this case, cutting the head off the snake would certainly leave the body to wither.

The former military commander did not trust anyone enough to be his successor and since his cause seemed purely selfish, he gave his subordinates only enough power to be useful at their tasks. Free thinking, according to reports, was discouraged for the most part. Yes, they were expected to make clever battle decisions but their objectives were handed down by Krilan himself and they were supposed to follow them.

No matter what.

A couple words caught Siva's attention and she paused the incoming data feed, peering at the phrase on the screen. She had to rewind, sliding back several paragraphs until she saw what she was after. A ship name, one she didn't expect to ever see again. *The Crystal Font*. They'd gone to a compromised research facility and hadn't been heard from since.

One of the buoys picked up a transmission and relayed it back to high command. Apparently, they were asking for some help. But it had been a *long* time since they were even heard from. What could've possibly happened? Were they stranded in some random system out in the middle of nowhere? How did they survive so long?

Siva brought up the ship's records and looked up the Anthar. Kale Ru'Xin, who had been recently promoted prior to his mission, led the ship. He'd been an exemplary officer and blazed through the ranks. High command considered the loss of him and his crew extremely regrettable and they'd all been listed as Missing in Action.

I guess that's no longer the case but if they truly do need help after this long, I don't think a normal military party is going to cut it. I need to intervene.

Siva put in her personal authorization code and claimed responsibility for the transmission, taking the mission away from the military. They'd complain, yes, but she didn't care. The Crystal Font could be a tremendous intelligence asset. If they managed to escape the attack on the research facility then survive alone out there for so long, she wanted them on *her* team.

After all, there were plenty of ships to conduct straight combat. She needed thinkers and survivors to conduct missions much like what the Behemoth had done. Those groups beyond the enemies at the gates, the rebels, pirates, terrorists and thugs wanting to bring down their government, those people needed opposition.

The Crystal Font would be perfect. Siva brought up their transmission to see where they were and what assistance they needed. Whatever she had to do to get them out of harm's way, she would but they sent quite the recording back. As she cued it up, she leaned back in her chair. Her mind began to formulate a plan even as she started up the personal log of Kale Ru'Xin.

Let's hope I'm not wrong about these folks and they weren't stuck out there due to incompetence. Well, if they were I'll spin it to say we saved them for the sake of their families and pull some good will for our efforts. Otherwise, I'm hoping we just drafted another ship into our cause. High command will be miffed but I think I can contend with them.

Okay, Kale. Show us what you've got. I'm sure this will be more than a little educational.

***

Chapter 1

Earlier...During the Research Facility Battle

Kale Ru'Xin cut the connection with the Behemoth and turned to Wena Fi'Devo, his communication's officer. He'd committed them to a daring, but possibly foolhardy act. The next phase of his plan involved pushing the young Zanthari's skills and he approached her station to assist as much as he'd be able.

"The enemy will be monitoring our coms," Kale explained. "I need you to send a desperate message to the Behemoth, something our ally's computer will immediately decode but the enemy will need at least a moment. I don't want it to seem too easy for them. Can you do it and ensure it looks good?"

Wena nodded, her orange eyes wide. "I believe so, sir. Yes."

"Good." Kale patted her shoulder. "Thank them for transferring the data from the research facility back to us and let them know we'll be taking it to another secret research facility on..." He hummed. "Xion Six."

"Sir?" Wena looked confused.

"What is it?"

"The Xion system is barely charted let alone..." Realization swept over her face. "Oh. I see the plan now."

"Excellent." Kale grinned. "Right away, please." He returned to his seat and directed his attention to Athan Du'Zhatha, the pilot. "I know you're already pushing the engines but I'm going to need a little more if at all possible. If my plan works, our jump out of here will be...theatrical to say the least."

"Um..." Athan glanced back, even as he worked. "What exactly does that mean?"

"When I finish talking to engineering, I'll let you know. For now, I need you to set a course for...Aelat. That's far enough away from here, and still in the other direction from Earth. When we get there, we'll redirect so get to working on those calculations."

Kale turned to Thaina, the weapon's officer. "Please don't make it too easy for them to keep up with us, huh?"

Thaina tilted her head and took to her controls, firing their turrets at the pursuing enemies. Kale did a quick check, noting every shot slammed the lead enemy vessel's bow. Their shields flared as some of the blasts went through, striking their hull and causing sparks to fly. She didn't let up, continuing to fire throughout.

Kale clicked over to engineering in the meantime. Su-Anthar Meira Di'Erran picked up immediately. "Yes, Anthar? I hope you're calling to let me know we can slow down now."

"I'm afraid not. I need you to help me pull off something I theorized about at the academy. A jump method that should get us out of here." Kale cleared his throat. "Can we expel engine waste and ignite it *during* a jump?"

Meira scoffed, her voice clearly showing serious disdain for the idea. "It's possible but beyond dangerous! There's a good chance it would go up before we left the system and that would disable our engines for sure. I assume that we're moving fast because we have to be and if that's the case, then stopping would definitely be detrimental to our survival."

"We have to pull a trick," Kale explained. "There's an entire enemy fleet on us. In fact, I've made sure they won't let up. Plus, I've given them a false impression of where we're going. I need to delay them so when we reappear, we'll have time to jump again. Believe me, this is a desperate hour so I'm going to need you to be as flexible and creative as you've ever been."

Meira hesitated for a long moment but finally let out a sigh. "Yes, I can do it. It'll take just a moment to prepare the purge but when I do it, we'll be ready to go. Do we have a course laid in and ready for the jump?"

Kale turned to Athan who nodded. "Yes, we're ready to go."

"Okay, begin the countdown," Meira said. "Twenty seconds and this will be one of the more spectacular things anyone will see this side of the galaxy."

"Thaina, I believe we can let up," Kale said. "Those cannons will spoil our plans if you keep shooting."

"Yes, sir." Thaina leaned back. "The lead ship has fallen back. They are firing at us but they're doing so half heartedly. I guess Wena's message worked."

"They want to disable us," Kale said. "They have no intention of losing what we've got. Not if they can help it."

Kale braced himself for their departure, prepared for the worst. They had to buy the

Behemoth time but he had no intention of sacrificing his ship without at least trying to get away. Much as he wanted to stick around and fight, the numbers were overwhelming. The data from the research facility might go a long way toward the war effort but it didn't have to come at the cost of *all* the alliance ships in that region.

The enemy started taking additional pot shots at them about half way through the countdown. Kale held his breath, hoping they'd be away before any appreciable damage came their way. Meira's voice crackled over the speakers near the tech officer, indicating the waste had been expelled. The highly volatile substance would cause a massive explosion the moment they initiated their jump.

If any enemy ships were too close, they'd likely go up but Kale couldn't hope for taking any of them out. All he wanted was the sensor interference such an event would cause, granting them time to get out of there. The theory earned him top marks in school but he'd never had an opportunity to implement the idea.

The exact right circumstances never came up until that moment. As he throttled the ship toward the dangerous maneuver, he closed his eyes for a moment, asking the fates to be kind. Not only to the Crystal Font but the Behemoth as well. They'd done a lot of great work together and he looked forward to seeing them again.

We made a good team. Please don't let this be the last time we're together.

"Initiating jump sequence now," Athan said. "Hang on, everyone. This will definitely be a little rough."

Kale held his breath as the ship began to hum. Something shook the entire vessel, nearly tossing him from his seat but it ended as swiftly as it began. A familiar sense of nothingness washed over him but instead of clearing up, it seemed to linger. He tried to inhale but his lungs would not respond. He couldn't close his eyes, couldn't divert his focus from the bright, white wall ahead of him.

Sound fled, all sensation lifted and he began to wonder if he'd crossed over. Had the ship exploded? Was he dead? Where was everyone else? Maybe the jump was simply taking longer than expected but they were supposed to be instantaneous. In all his years in space, he'd never spent more than a few, brief moments in such a state.

How long can this possibly last? Forever, I suppose...though it's not as comforting as I always thought it would be. Why would it be? It became harder to think, harder to cling to his identity, difficult to even *be* but he knew if he let go, he might never come back. Kale struggled but deep down he recognized the futility of fighting.

I can't give up...I won't...no matter what.

***

The Present

Clea An'Tufal sat in her quarters as they approached her home world, excited for an opportunity to relax after their recent mission. Despite her sincere desire to get out and finish the war, having been involved in a major action to stop the civil conflict left her somewhat spent. Her own people had faced such strife in their past and she knew what it could do to a people.

Though she knew they wouldn't have a lot of down time, the opportunity to put her feet on solid, safe ground sounded like a tremendous luxury. She had reached out to her parents to see if they would be available to see her but she discovered they were both away on their own assignments, away from the capital. Clea wouldn't have time to visit them but then again, she'd seen them a great deal the last couple times she was there.

A night in her family apartment wouldn't go amiss, even if it happened to be alone.

She checked the chronometer and saw she had several hours left before they'd dock, plenty to catch a nap. Her shift started when they arrived but Captain Gray Atwell already gave her leave to go planet side. She took a deep breath and started to doze just as her computer started dinging, indicating an incoming message.

"Clea," Gray said. "I've got an incoming transmission from Siva. She needs to talk to you and I directly."

Really? I was almost asleep! Can't this wait? All the thoughts drifted through her head but instead of voicing her annoyance, she merely tapped the receive button and said, "I'll be there momentarily."

Crawling out of her bunk, she put her uniform back on, straightened her hair the best she could and headed for the Captain's office. There, they'd find out what the next unreasonable ask intelligence had for them. Clea preferred straight forward action. She hated having to lie to the various crew members about their last mission and they still hadn't been able to tell those involved what they were really doing there.

Stopping the civil war was a fringe benefit to Siva's real aim. She probably didn't really care about the novalat people at all but had to play nice with high command. I don't like this woman much at all.

Clea knocked at Gray's door and he called for her to enter. She stepped inside and straightened her jacket before moving to the seat. He looked almost as tired as she felt. Had he tried to catch some rest as well? Wouldn't surprise her considering what they'd been up to as of late but their duty seemed to be unwilling to give them a reprieve.

Gray started the conversation, "do you have any idea what she might want?"

Clea shook her head. "I'm afraid not. Probably another crazy mission. You know, I find it somewhat frustrating intelligence has operational control over our ship. I'm shocked your government handed it over."

"They were playing nice," Gray explained. "Plus, don't forget we missed the Christening of our new ship. They've got a defender even if they're green. There are worse ways to serve. So long as we get our crack at the front lines when we invade our enemy's space, I'm fine with wherever they send us."

"You might not feel that way after this conversation." Clea finally grinned. "If you don't mind my saying."

"Now you've got me nervous." Gray tapped the computer. "Here we go." A few moments passed as they established a connection. Siva's image appeared on the screen and she grinned up at both of them.

"You have to love this FTL communication, huh? Works great. How're you doing?"

"Uh...we're great?" Gray shrugged. "What can we do for you?"

Siva nodded. "Right to the point. That works for me. Very well, here we go. I've got some news for you before we get to my point. First up, Miss An'Tufal. I believe you were promised a rather prestigious title and were merely made a Su-Anthar. Mei'Gora couldn't go all the way but you needed something to tide you over I guess."

Clea hadn't even thought about her rank since she achieved it. Even as Siva brought it up, she was surprised. Considering everything going on, their work and missions, she didn't find it important. Regardless of what title they put before her name, she planned to continue serving for as long as it took.

Even after the war ended, she wanted to continue to be part of the military, hopefully as they turned to an exploratory path. Rank might not mean nearly as much then as it did during the duress of action. She looked forward to the future, knowing she didn't have the overt danger of weapons being fired at the vessel she crewed.

But until then, and at that moment, she was in the present with a war to win and another assignment offered by the intelligence division. *Here we go.*

"I didn't think it really mattered, ma'am," Clea said. "We've had bigger things to deal with."

"Sure. Regardless, I've been authorized to upgrade your status and grant you the rank of Tathin. Congratulations...though you should've already had it. Thank you for your service, Miss An'Tufal."

Gray smiled. "Yes, congratulations."

Clea struggled not to roll her eyes and simply accepted the honor with a nod. "Thank you, ma'am. I appreciate it."

"Excellent! Let's move along." Siva leaned forward and hit a button, reading from a screen. "Second up, I wanted to tell you that Earth sent a message stating that they've got their third ship moving along quickly. Our fabrication techniques are doing them right. Thought you'd like to know. Oh! Personnel. Maury Higgins has recovered from his wounds and is currently helping with some of the building."

"That's great news," Gray said. "I've been worried about him."

"I think he wants to come back to the Behemoth," Siva said, "but considering Durant's taken his job, he'll probably have to settle for working with the newer crews back in your home system. At least for now. By the way, High Command tried to get Durant reassigned to one of their research facilities but I denied that and ensured he'll stay on with you."

"That's unexpectedly kind of you," Gray said. "May I ask why?"

"I need my crews to be the best," Siva replied, "which leads me to the real reason we're talking over the com rather than in person. I wanted to give you this information right away so you'd know that time is going to be precious. When you've returned and provisioned, we're going to have to send you right back out."

Clea stiffened but kept her mouth shut.

"What's the assignment?"

Siva's eyes twinkled. "I think you're going to like it. Do you remember *The Crystal Font*? Alliance ship you went to the research facility with?"

"Of course," Gray said. "How could we forget? Kale Ru'Xin sacrificed his ship to let us escape with the data...or so we thought."

"Turns out he didn't but...there's a complication."

"Of course there is," Clea muttered.

"You see, we know for a fact that the ship was not destroyed. We received a transmission recently bounced through multiple buoys. It appears they were able to get out of the system through a risky maneuver and were lost for a time. I'm hoping you can help us get them back. Specifically, I want them to come back and work with my team."

"Adding to the roster?" Gray asked.

"So to speak. Anyone as clever as Kale and his crew are people I need. I heard you worked well together out there so I assumed you'd like to know someone capable has your back. After all, intelligence rarely has someone they can send for backup. Believe me, they need some right now."

"I'll help them, of course," Gray said. "Anything I can do. We owe them big."

"Not to put too fine a point on it, and just in the interest of keeping things transparent," Siva paused and let out a sigh. "Well...you didn't really have a choice. I suppose we could've allowed you to feel like you did with that last statement but ultimately, you're under my operational command and I need you to find *The Crystal Font* as soon as possible."

It was Gray's turn to stiffen. Clea saw the muscles tighten in his neck but his expression did not change. He nodded once. "Understood."

"Fantastic! Let's go back to being friends. It's a lot more pleasant. Anyway, I'll see you both when you get back to the planet. We'll have drinks and talk. Then, you can take off and save your friends. Bring them back and let them re-join the cause. I'm pretty sure they're going to have a wild story to tell. Talk soon!"

Siva broke the connection and Gray shook his head.

"She's got a lot of nerve."

Clea nodded. "She does indeed. I wondered when she was remind us of her power and influence. I suppose that was the time."

"Indeed." Gray stood up and moved to the window, peering out. "I am happy we have the chance to help Kale. I can't believe he survived. The man is incredible."

"I always figured he was too wily to go down the way we thought." Clea rubbed her eyes. "I only hope he and his crew are in the condition to do what she's asking. I can promise you this: if our actions turn out to be little more than charity, Siva won't be pleased."

Gray shrugged. "What can she do about it? For our part, we're going to save those people regardless of their use to intelligence. I think we owe them that much, huh?"

"Yes, we do." Clea stood up. "Shall I call a briefing of the senior staff?"

"Please." Gray didn't turn. "Make it for an hour. Should give us plenty of time for debate before we put into port. And hopefully, with any luck we'll get some rest before heading back out to the unknown."

"I guess that's what we do now. Plunge into the unknown."

"If we weren't at war, I'd feel a lot more comfortable about that," Gray said. "For now, we'll do what we can. See you in an hour, Clea."

"Yes, sir." Clea left the room and turned to her computer, setting up the requested meeting. She figured everyone would be chomping at the bit to help *The Crystal Font*, especially after the valor they displayed in their previous mission. With any luck, they'd find them in good health and ready to rejoin the fleet.

The alternative was too tragic to think about.

***

Gray continued staring out the window long after Clea left. He thought about Kale needing help and it filled him with a sense of urgency. After the jump disaster which thrust them into a first contact situation, he had a full understanding of how bad space travel could go wrong. The Behemoth couldn't call for help but it would've been nice.

If Siva had some coordinates, Gray was willing to jump out there right away but the fact she didn't offer them made him feel like there had to be a catch. Some bad news was waiting for them when they arrived and met with her. At least the woman had confidence Kale and his crew were okay.

Gray wondered if Siva would've told them about *The Crystal Font* if she didn't think they were worth joining intelligence. She probably would've let high command take care of it and that meant kielan ships. They wouldn't have turned to the Behemoth, not for something involving one of their own.

They might all be part of the same alliance but that didn't mean there weren't fraternities. In fact, the military leaders might not be too thrilled they were being cut out of the chance to find their friends. Gray hoped he wouldn't have to deal with any of that type of rivalry or cold shoulder. Someone was going to save those people. That should be enough.

Yet deep down, Gray really wanted to be the person that made it out there, that got to the ship first and made a difference. Much as he wanted everyone to take the high road, he understood if someone felt resentment. Leaving the Crystal Font at the end of that mission was one of the hardest things he'd done and he thought about Kale a lot.

Their roles could've been reversed. Gray thought about responsibility a lot and how a commander might find himself in a position where all the lives and people counting on him might mean less than the objective. Much as he wanted to believe he'd never have to weigh sacrificing his ship for a mission, Kale was a sharp reminder it might happen some day.

What a terrible thing to consider. During that engagement, Kale could've gotten away. We were facing the engine trouble. All he had to do was jump out. Lucky for us, he paused and asked some questions but we were leaving. This next mission is personal. Much like Clea's treasure hunt, I have to bring Kale home.

Considering what the kielan commander did for them, Gray knew Kale would do the same. The man's first command alone made quite the impression on everyone. Gray never heard if they gave him a funeral or not. He didn't know how they treated people who were considered missing in action. At what point would they be declared dead?

Maybe no one wanted to give up on them. The idea they *could* still be alive might be compelling enough to leave the books open. Kielans seemed to need proof of a deed before they believed it. Even the logs of the Behemoth probably weren't enough to convince them that *The Crystal Font* was destroyed.

After all, even Clea said that it could've just been a spectacular jump.

I hope it was. Maybe that's why they've been unable to communicate for so long. God knows where they ended up.

The Behemoth's own jump disaster took them into occupied space but there were plenty of systems which held nothing at all. If anyone planned to survive in those places, they would need to be resourceful. Especially if they were unable to use their jump drive again. Whatever Kale and his crew did to survive and escape must've caused some serious damage.

Otherwise, they'd bring themselves home.

The thought of them returning all on their own made Gray smile. Depending on their story, they could be considered heroes, men and women of extreme resourcefulness. An inspiration to the rest of the military getting ready to fight a massive war. The benefit of such an event didn't mean as much as surviving.

They were all a team so Gray wouldn't have felt any shame having someone come to their aid. The Kielans did that for them when the enemy invaded Sol. Humans accepted a lot of assistance over the last few years. It was one of the reasons that Gray never felt indignant about performing tasks for the alliance.

In many ways, humanity owed them a little military service. Helping out meant they had the opportunity to experience the rest of the galaxy, opening their eyes to just how small Earth truly was. It also allowed them to settle some of their debt to the people who saved their planet and all their lives.

Many people on board the Behemoth were there the day they were beset upon by the enemy and remembered the kielan warships that showed up and fought them off. They remember when Clea came on board and began to help them build their first pulse drive to leave the solar system.

Isolationists were a loud faction on Earth but fortunately, they represented a small part of the population. Most people understood what they'd been given, that none of them would be alive had it not been for the alliance. Without even leaving the planet, many people were able to fathom the gravity of what that enemy represented and as a result, they embraced the galactic union of many races.

Those who didn't, mostly close minded bigots, felt they should conduct their own battle. They lived on pure emotion, never bothering to use logic to recognize any culture standing alone in the face of the enemy would surely perish. And badly. Gray had seen them up close and personal on several occasions and he knew Earth needed allies.

So many people continue to fear the unknown, even in our allies. I suspect Commander Everly leans in that direction as well. All those years working alongside Clea hasn't dampened his feelings against the alliance. I suspect he feels like we should be leading this group rather than taking orders. He doesn't realize how much experience these people bring to the table in regards to space exploration, defense and combat.

Whether Adam truly believed in the inferiority of the alliance or not, he kept it to himself. However, Gray noted quips here and there that gave him the impression. He hoped his executive officer might come around but some feelings, some views were harder to squash than others. Even exposed to the greater universe, encountering factions like Orion's Light, didn't necessarily change minds.

Like the traitors we had to deal with. Not only Clea's sister but in our own crew members as well. The sabotage that nearly killed us all and the idiotic council member who honestly thought murdering the entire ship sounded like a solid plan.

Gray's computer reminded him he had fifteen minutes before his pre-briefing. He wanted everyone to be thinking about the part they had to play in their next assignment. They didn't have a lot of information yet, but each department needed to be prepared for what was to come. He knew some of his senior staff took leaving Kale's people behind harder than others, specifically the marines.

We have a chance to make it right. Gray left his office, heading out to join the others. The moment he entered the briefing room, he'd set in motion a flurry of activity, giving the entire crew a great deal to do. They'd been idling, likely thinking about what they were going to do next, perhaps even dwelling on the major battle to come.

At least this will distract them from possibilities. None of them needs negativity right now and this upcoming mission is nothing if not positive.

***

Clea stepped out of the briefing with Commander Adam Everly and Group Commander Estaban Revente. The two men looked dour, their eyes narrow with thought, brows furrowed in concentration. They stopped just outside the door and remained silent for several moments before Adam finally spoke up.

"I can't believe they made it."

"Glorious survival instincts," Revente said. "I don't know how they did it, of course, but whatever got them out of that mess had to be ingenious."

Clea added, "the likeliest possibility is that they did something with their jump drive to mask their signature. Maybe overloaded part of their engine. It would explain why they couldn't get back on their own. Remember when we thought they might've blown up? An overload definitely has the power to cause such a flash."

Adam nodded. "Interesting. Good on them." He turned to Revente. "Sounds like your folks are going to be doing some recon work finally. I'll bet they look forward to not having to shoot at something for a change."

"You have no idea," Revente replied. "My teams could definitely use a break from getting out there. Inertial dampeners only do so much. Their bodies are taking a beating every time they engage in those dogfights. Some of them are going to have to retire a lot earlier than I'm sure they'll want to as a result."

"Harsh." Adam shook his head. "Supposedly, we only have one major battle left."

"Um…" Clea cleared her throat before continuing. "Even if we win the war, we've got Orion's Light to contend with…among other problems. Those fringe factions out there aren't going to go away with the enemy. The only good news is we'll be able to focus all of our attention on them and that means, they won't have long to operate."

"Fair point," Revente said. "But I have a feeling our friends at the Orion's Light aren't going to be a huge problem after the real enemy's gone. After all, they can't possibly field a fleet as large as the alliance. With all our members? Impossible. We'd overwhelm them with sheer numbers."

"But that's not how they operate, is it?" Clea asked. "No, they're guerrilla fighters, causing disorder like in the Novalat system or harassing colonies as they did while looking for the artifact. We're dealing with total scum here and they have absolutely no rules. Even though they came from my people, they have truly cast off any of our values."

"Cheery thought," Adam muttered. "But we'll be ready for them. Revente, do you need anything from me?"

Revente shook his head. "I'm on my way to brief my people. I'll be fine. Thanks for the chat. We'll talk again when we make port."

"Good. See you then." Adam turned to Clea. "What about you? Are you good?"

"I don't have anyone to brief," Clea grinned. "I'm going to take the nap I was trying to indulge before we got the call about this mission. I'll see you on the bridge in a while, huh?"

"Indeed." Adam nodded and left her alone.

Clea returned to her quarters, rubbing her eyes as she got to the door. Some days, she got the impression Adam merely tolerated her where others, he seemed friendly. She never understood where she stood with him but ultimately didn't care. They were part of a team and she felt she had no choice but to make their situation work to the best of her ability.

Did the Commander have a problem with kielans? Or the alliance in general? Possibly. Some humans didn't trust them and she partially understood. After making contact with dozens of alien races, Clea knew what suspicion looked like. Other cultures worried that the alliance wanted something from them they couldn't necessarily give.

What if the alliance simply took the resources they needed or kidnapped people? Most of the cultures they initially met wouldn't have been able to do anything about it. Perhaps those people would've felt better if the kielan people *had* been more aggressive. Kindness sometimes felt like buttering up…preparing them for some hidden agenda.

The Novalat people discovered quickly that they were being welcomed into a collective rather than treated as some kind of commodity. They even remarked on it publicly once, thanking the alliance for their patience and indulgence in what amounted to growing pains. Some of the others were less noble about admitting it but they tended to come around.

Would humanity? Some of them had, or at least made a good show of it. Clea studied enough of their history to know they could be clever, outright devious even. Their Machiavelli taught them all sorts of things about how to be underhanded in politics. Depending on how nefarious their leaders were, they may well be trying to take a larger role, perhaps even trying to lead, the entire alliance.

Something told Clea that Siva knew this and probably already infiltrated the Earth's government. If she hadn't, she must've been in the process of trying. Getting someone in there, able to really watch them and stay involved, might save the partnership the entire alliance was founded upon. The last thing they need was to be dictated to by total amateurs in the galactic theater.

You're still not ready for some things, humanity. Be patient and you will be but we've been at this a long time. Don't think we're going to simply let you have the wheel because you're underhanded and sneaky. It pained Clea to think about it in such a way, especially since people like Gray were so reasonable.

But then she thought about the council member who betrayed them and her blood boiled a bit. The man tried to sacrifice *all* the people on board the Behemoth simply to discredit the alliance. His traitors turned on their friends, their comrades and essentially ruined their own lives in the process. For if they failed and survived, which they did, they looked forward to dying in prison.

I can't even imagine accepting such an assignment. One of the men, their navigator, threw away a brilliant career. Astrogation had been his passion. He knew so much about the stars. Clea spent hours talking to him about astronomy and helped boost his understanding of the concepts through her own experiences.

Kielan education on the subject vastly exceeded what one could learn in a human school.

And despite all their time together, he was still able to make the decision to help sabotage the ship and nearly kill them. He ultimately turned on his fellow traitors and put the entire thing to rest but it didn't exonerate him from his fate. Maybe he got a few less years, or some privileges in prison as a result but none of those three were walking away.

That's what happens when you decide your agenda outweighs your friends. Clea flopped on the bed, not even bothering to take her jacket off. She closed her eyes and let out a deep breath, trying not to think of Vora An'Tufal, her sister. That was the ultimate form of blind, stupid betrayal.

Vora didn't even side with some fringe part of the alliance but rather, the enemy itself. She led them straight to the research facility and got countless people killed. The government took her away and Clea hadn't heard what happened to her. She thought about asking Siva but didn't want to sound overly concerned.

The last thing she wanted was to be looked at as a potential traitor.

Luckily, kielan justice tended to focus solely on the criminal and not blame the family members or close friends. Otherwise, Clea would never have received the Tathin promotion. Much as family meant to their people and how close they all were, when a bad apple revealed itself, it was simply removed and everyone else moved on.

My parents sure aren't thrilled about it. In private, during her last visit, they talked about missing Vora. It was an emotional conversation, one they probably needed. None of them asked the obvious questions of how or why Vora could betray her people. The stated reason didn't help, that of them losing anyway. Nihilism didn't become a brilliant scientist and yet, she embraced the philosophy.

Clea wondered about her own future with the military. What did she really want to do? Eventually, the Behemoth would have to return to the Earth and they would likely no longer need her. They probably didn't already considering their service to the alliance. Still, she enjoyed her time with them and wanted to remain, at least until the overall objectives were complete.

The thought of going back to her own people filled her with mixed emotions. On one hand, she missed being amongst people who intrinsically understood her without having to *learn* her culture. On the other, she'd developed quite a few positive relationships amongst the humans.

Having Durant around helped. He might've been wildly eccentric but at least he grew up in the same way. Clea spent a lot of time with him, working through puzzles and problems involving weapons and the technology that made the Behemoth go. Would she continue in such a capacity somewhere else?

The Tathin rank offered many possibilities. Though she might never command a ship, she could run operations or even a tech division. She felt especially suited for such a task. Still, high command would have to pick the assignment and she only hoped she'd have some say before they simply stuck her somewhere.

After everything she did, all the sacrifices she made to leave home and live with the humans, she felt her own people owed her. Perhaps such entitlement was unfair and until she knew for sure, she'd keep it to herself but when the time came, if her new job didn't suit her, she'd definitely play some cards.

Maybe Siva could even help. Much as Clea didn't like the woman, she figured the spy master might owe her a favor too. Such people were good to keep close and not alienate. They held so much influence, they could take a starship out of active rotation and send it on random missions.

If Intelligence happened to be her future, as long as she wasn't a deep cover operative, Clea could see herself thriving in the environment. Analyzing tech data or even helping to collect it from the safety of a starship made sense to her.

What she didn't want was to undergo some kind of spy training and infiltrate enemy factions.

She'd performed a couple of ground operations and found it stressful beyond belief. Especially after receiving an injury. Clea could fight and defend herself but that was a far cry from the types of things intelligence operatives were expected to do. They were straight killers and for her, she only wanted to pull the trigger when absolutely necessary.

Only people like Siva put you in the position to make that question an easy one to answer. Shoot or be shot. I don't need it. In any event, I need to stop thinking and start sleeping. We'll be at the port before I even got a half hour. The chime went off stating they were rapidly approaching the space station. The reminder gave her fifteen minutes before she needed to be on the bridge.

Damn it, brain! You are not *working with me today!* Clea got up and changed her jacket to something that wasn't wrinkled, heading for the bridge. Exhaustion closed in on her but she knew she'd get some sleep when they got to the planet. She only had to work for another couple hours before then. *I'm going to hit the pillow like a pulse bomb.*

Clea leaned against the wall on the elevator and closed her eyes, hoping Kale and his crew were okay. *We'll be there soon,* she thought. *Hang in there…we won't leave you alone. Not this time.*

Chapter 2

Kale opened his eyes, staring at the pilot's console sideways. He was lying on the floor in front of the Anthar's chair, his muscles numb and his ears ringing. This happened before, he'd been in this exactly position. It was before his promotion, during a conflict that took his mentor's life. Once again, he found himself barely conscious, struggling to regain his senses.

Are we in immediate danger? Straining to hear, he didn't make out any sounds of concern or stress. The ship remained motionless, no shaking from impacts nor did the engine make the vessel tremble. Feeling returned to his arms and he pushed himself into a sitting position, blinking blurry eyes in an effort to take in his surroundings.

Others stirred, his bridge crew each coming around in the same slow manner Kale recovered. He swallowed, wincing at how parched he felt. His whole body screamed for a drink but he needed to take the concerns one step at a time. Assessing the threat around them and finding out where they were, those were the priorities.

"Is anyone at their post?" Kale's question came out as a croak and he cleared his throat, trying to find his voice. When he tried again, he spoke with more strength. "Anyone?"

"I'm up," Athan replied and Kale watched as the pilot reclaimed his seat. "Looks like the computers are rebooting, sir."

"Thank you." Kale grabbed hold of his chair and hoisted himself into it, settling back as his heart raced and his entire body complained about the exertion. *If this keeps up, I'll need to visit the doctor. Lord, that place is going to be a nightmare if everyone feels like I do.* "When you know our position, report. I'd like some scans...find out if we're alone. Wherever we are."

"Anthar," Deva Thi'Noch, his tech officer, spoke up. She sounded worried. "I...think we might have some data corruption. I'm working on repairing it but..."

"What is it?" Kale asked, with more bite than he intended.

"Um...it's just...well, it can't be right."

"What can't be?" Kale rubbed his eyes. "Just spit it out."

"The time, sir." Deva sighed. "The computer *insists* that we have been in our current position for over a month."

"Impossible." Kale waved his hand at her. "You're right, there's corruption somewhere in there. How's it even verifying that?"

"There's a buoy nearby. It's transmitter seems to be out but it's still keeping accurate time." Deva shrugged. "I suppose *it* could've been damaged."

"That's your answer," Kale said. "Anyway, scan the entire system and get a damage report on that buoy. I have a feeling we're going to need to call for help and if that thing's broken, we'll have to fix it. Athan, do you have our position?"

"We're drifting, sir." Athan shrugged. "I'll have engine control when the reboot finishes but for now, I have no idea where we are. This isn't a star that I'm familiar with. I'm checking the charts...this *must* have been surveyed or there wouldn't be a buoy, right?"

"Not necessarily," Deva replied. "Some of those were sent out as deep space probes, programmed to locate out of the way systems to assist wayward ships...like ours. They don't necessarily mean anyone's been here before. They just anticipate arrival in case someone gets stranded."

"I read about that," Kale said. "Either way, it won't matter. We'll get it online and report in. Once we fix our data corruption." He tapped his console. "Engineering, this is the Anthar, do you copy?"

No response came back.

"Engineering, this is Anthar Ru'Xin, do you read me?"

Still no response.

"Someone must've rebooted everything," Athan said. "They had to have initiated it."

Deva nodded. "You're right. Automation was offline. Only life support was functioning and even that was operating on the emergency generator."

Kale's body finally began to return to normal and he was able to stand without feeling dizzy. Still, he kept a steady hand on the chair and took several deep breaths. When he felt confident he would not topple over, he stepped over to the communication station where Wena was just getting to her seat.

"You okay?" He asked her and she nodded. "Good. First thing's first. Coordinate with the other departments throughout the ship. Make sure you get a full report of damage and casualties. Start with medical. They're probably going to be the busiest for a bit. I'm heading down to engineering to see what's going on."

"Sir, is that wise?" Deva asked. "I haven't finished scanning our structural integrity yet. It might not be safe."

"I'll take the chance," Kale said. "Someone had to have done it and if there was a hull breach, they wouldn't have been able to. Besides, we seem to be steady and our drift is pretty light. I think we're in better shape than we should be."

"Yes, sir." Deva nodded. "I'll continue to compile information."

"Thank you." Kale stepped onto the elevator. "Keep me informed through personal com, just in case ship wide is out. Stay focused on your tasks at hand and we'll get out of here in short order."

The doors closed and Kale leaned back against the wall, closing his eyes. The downward motion made his stomach turn. Nausea lasted only a moment before settling into a general discomfort. He forced himself to consider their predicament, pushing aside his physical ailments in light of the mystery of where they were and how they got there.

Jump accidents were a common topic at the academy. Every astrogation class, from beginner to advance, talked about the mishaps throughout history. Some of them were outright horrifying, to the point Kale was surprised anyone stayed in the military after they read about them. He wasn't entirely sure when he came to terms with the possibilities and accepted them but everyone he served with must've done the same.

Instructors always tried to couch their lectures with the fact that safety protocols had dramatically increased since the first jump drives were introduced. Back then, *parts* of ships might disappear, ensuring both sides were destroyed. Some simply exploded. Others ignored the courses input into their systems, appearing *inside* objects.

An old regulation stated no ship was to jump directly to the home world. Even with every safety protocol in place, they were to show up on the edge of the system and fly in through conventional engines. Since that particular little rule never left the books, some should've still been worried but until a potential mishap occurred, one didn't really think about it anymore.

This may not have been a mishap so much as damage, Kale thought. *The explosion from the waste could've seriously impacted our engines. Wait!*

Kale's eyes snapped open seconds before the doors slid to the sides. He stepped off and leaned against the wall in the hallway as his memory trickled back. The brief moment of nothingness he'd experienced plenty of times through jumps lasted *much* longer than ever before. He remembered fighting it...trying to breathe...trying not to give in to the terror of lingering in that state.

The Fates certainly tested us all. I wonder when the rest of the crew will recall that struggle. We won't be able to jump again until we can run enough tests to ensure we don't have a repeat performance.

The engineering deck tended to have a great deal of activity in the area but as he refocused his attention, he noted no one was moving around in the hall. He paced toward the door, his footsteps echoing overhead. The scene felt eerie and he fended off a feeling of dread, like he might find something horrible.

As he drew closer to the door, he heard voices and a weight from his heart lifted. He tapped the panel and input his personal code, granting him access. Someone drew a firearm and aimed it at him before they seemed to recognize him. The security guard immediately lowered his weapon.

"Anthar!" The young man pressed his hand against his chest in a salute. "Forgive me, we had no idea what was going on!"

"Thank you for not shooting me, Zanthari," Kale said. "Where's Engineer Di'Erran?"

"She's with the other seniors," the guard said, pointing deeper into the engine room. "They're checking the crystals."

Kale looked at the other engineers, each working on some task at a terminal. He picked one at random, a vinthari he didn't know. The young man must've joined them just before they headed to Earth. He stepped over and watched his efforts, noting he was working on regulating power throughout the ship. The generators needed some coaxing to properly balance the load when first turned back on.

"Can you give me a report, Vinthari?"

The young man didn't look up and continued to work. "Yes, sir. When we came to, we were on backup power. The only systems still functioning at normal levels were life support and environmental shields. Those are on backup generators, totally detached from the main engines. We reignited the generators after a systems check and rebooted all systems."

"Are there any problems left for us to worry about then?"

"Chief Engineer Di'Erran is concerned about the crystals. They might be damaged, which would mean we're stuck here until we can fit a replacement. And that's if the setting is alright. Also, our regulators are down or I wouldn't have to be ensuring power doesn't surge through the system. The last thing we need right now is a bunch of shorts. Especially since medical just called down and demanded more power."

"Understood. What's the ETA for full power?"

"I wish I could give you a good estimate, sir. Most stations are operating at nominal levels, providing they don't tap them out with regular usage. I'll have a proper time frame soon though, and will certainly let you know."

"Thank you." Kale smiled, patting him on the shoulder. "I appreciate your efforts. Carry on without me distracting you." He stepped away, observing each station in turn. Nothing appeared to be damaged, which gave him a good feeling of how lucky they were. The engines *could* have taken a serious beating considering what they did and he wouldn't have been surprised if he showed up to fires and chaos.

Instead, he found a calm crew doing their jobs to the best of their abilities. Kale couldn't be more proud of their tenacity and professionalism. Considering Meira literally dove back into her job the second she was up said a lot about her dedication as well. He'd buy her a drink when they got back to the home world.

And that's just a matter of time. First, however, we need to get everything fixed up and safe for our departure.

Kale plunged deeper into the engineering room, heading for the crystal chamber. At the end of the hall, he saw Meira working with several others, moving about checking panels and screens. They shouted back and forth, relaying the information they found as a person on the edge took notes.

Meira paused when she noticed Kale. "Hold up," she said to her crew. "Continue to collect the data. I'll be back with you in a moment."

"This looks dire," Kale said as she approached. "How're we doing?"

"Which part?" Meira scratched the back of her neck. "All primary systems will be back online and functional after the reboot is complete. A few circuits went and we've got individual, secondary units that require attention but they can wait. Our biggest problem is the jump drive and crystal assembly. I'm afraid the gem might be cracked."

Kale winced. Everyone who attended the academy knew about pulse drives and how they garnered power from their perfectly cut crystal's vibrations. It fed the generators and maintained a constant and clean power stream for the entire ship. Cracked didn't mean it wouldn't give them energy but the sheer amount required for a jump would probably make it break outright.

Which would likely result in their immediate destruction.

"What're we looking at?"

"Replacement," Meira said. "Which we can do. We've got the back up stored away but as you know, that takes time. And when I bring the pulse drive offline to do it, we'll be on generator power for the better part of two shifts. We'll need to be on severe conservation throughout just in case there are any delays in getting it back online."

"Understood." Kale hummed. "How long before you think we can begin the process?"

Meira sighed. "Another hour before we're back up to full power and all generators are restored to full strength. We're still performing a risk analysis and ensuring we can even take the thing out without impacting the assembly. If that's cracked or damaged, we might be done. I hope you were able to get a message out."

"There's a buoy but we're not sure if it's even going to work." Kale shrugged. "We're trying either way. Can you give us sensors? There may be something in the area that can help us. A habitable planet or moon. We have thrusters until you take the engine offline, right?"

"Yes, you could move us now if you have to." Meira stepped closer and lowered her voice. "I'm mostly worried about the enemy. If they tracked us, we're going to be totally vulnerable to attack. There won't be anything we can do."

"I know but..." Kale shook his head. "Did you happen to note the date?"

"Yes, I'm looking into data corruption from our angle but Deva already let me know she's on it." Meira checked her tablet. "It can't be right...can it?"

"I don't know but if it is, then we may not have to worry about the enemy chasing us. They would've found us already."

"If we truly were sleeping for a month, then that was some profound stasis. What if we were midjump the whole time?" Meira smirked. "I don't have time to speculate like this but we might want to get a team in the briefing room to discuss at some point. I'm thinking there's some science here I'm missing...some precedent for what we might've experienced."

"If there is, I haven't heard about it," Kale replied. "I studied astrogation and jump behavior, too. No records I found or reported on talked about stasis or being trapped in the middle of one. Of course, there are countless reports of ships simply disappearing and never being seen again. It's more than possible one of them experienced what we did and simply could not get home."

"Cheery thought." Meira gestured back at the crystal. "With your permission, I'll get back to work."

"Please." Kale gestured. "Can you let me know where you're at soon?"

"We're making progress so it won't be long. Probably before you get settled back on the bridge."

"I'm heading to medical now to check on anyone who might've been hurt. Watch out for a briefing meeting. I'll have one sent out. Thanks for everying, Meira. Keep it up."

Kale returned to the elevator and rode it up two floors. There, he disembarked and paced down the hall toward the medical center. As he rounded the corner, he stopped in his tracks. People were lined up in the hallway, waiting for a turn to speak to a doctor. He approached and checked several of them over, most displaying too much fatigue to even note who he was.

They don't appear to be physically harmed but our re-entry must've done a number on them the way it had us. I'm guessing those closer to the hull got it the worst but who's to say what impacted them more than anyone else? We're going to need all essential personnel back to operational status as soon as possible.

Kale shouldered his way into the room and noted the controlled chaos going on within. Luckily, everyone was too exhausted to make much noise but the doctors moved about in a flurry of activity. They seemed to not be bad off but he figured they did something to themselves to operate at a normal level.

Kale approached the chief physician, Eirkan Ni'Otha, and tapped him gently on the shoulder. The older man jumped, turned and his irritable expression melted to one of resignation. He moved aside with the Anthar and kept his voice low, greeting him with a nod and muttered *hello*.

"This looks bad," Kale said. "Are there any injuries or is this some kind of strange fatigue?"

"They're exhausted, some to the point of near death," Eirkan said. "I've been issuing stimulants to the worst of them and having those totally spent get some sleep. We didn't seem as impacted by it in here and you seem okay." He ran a scanner over Kale. "Yes, you're reading tired but well."

"That's a relief," Kale replied. "I'm not sure how this happened but it looks like it effected the entire ship. Do you need anything else or do you have this under control?"

Eirkan sighed. "To the best of our ability, we do. We'll get everyone either in a bed or out of here in the next couple hours. Are there any personnel that you need sooner?"

"I might." Kale looked around. "I'll let you know and we can fast track them. Thanks for the update. I'll let you get back to work."

"Wait! What's going on with the engines? When're we going home?"

Kale offered him a worried grin. "I'm afraid that's another problem we're dealing with. I'll address the crew when we know more. For now, focus on the wounded. I'll take care of the rest." He paused to look over the various patients, letting out a sigh. Many of them were young, Zantharis on their first or second tour. It made his heart sting to see them suffer. "Good luck."

Heading back to the bridge, Kale was bombarded by information the moment he stepped off the elevator. He held up his hands. "Calm down. One at a time, please." He gestured to Deva, who seemed the most desperate to update him. "You first. Report."

"Captain, scans have picked up some strange readings on a nearby planet…like nothing I've seen before." Deva paused to catch her breath. "At first, I was convinced I was just picking up some kind of interference from the atmosphere or maybe even leakage from our engines but as I established more data, I discovered a constant and consistent emanation. It's definitely *not* natural. It *must* have been constructed."

"And you don't know what sort of technology might've brought this about?" Kale asked. "No idea who might be responsible?"

Deva shook her head. "No, sir! We have nothing like it on any database of the alliance. I don't even have a way to measure what it can do yet but I'm working on it."

"So what makes it so special?"

"The consistency and the fact that I'm detecting no radiation...no heat signature. Just a constant flow of power without venting." Deva shook her head. "It's impossible. Unless whatever created it found a way to re-harness the waste, I can't even begin to guess at how they're doing it. I need to get with the engineering team to look at my findings."

"One step at a time," Kale replied. "For now, continue your solo work on it and get me more information. The engineering staff remains busy. Is the planet habitable?"

Deva nodded, "yes, sir though I'd recommend hazard suits to be on the safe side.

There are readings I don't recognize…some kind of atmospheric anomaly."

"Okay. Get back to work." Kale turned to Athan. "What've you got?"

"Engineering let me know we have full power for now. However, if they're going to take the engines down we're going to need to get wherever we want to be for a while. If we're going to orbit this planet that Deva's on about, we need to get moving. Our plotted course will take a shift to arrive."

Kale nodded. "Let's get moving then. Just in case there's a good reason to be nearby." He turned his attention to Wena. "Did the buoy pan out?"

"I can't say one way or another," Wena said. "I didn't get any log back for success or failure. It is orbiting the planet and maintaining itself just fine…though it makes no sense. It's engines seem to be offline. Something's holding it up there and I don't know what. In any event, I recommend we attempt to perform maintenance on the buoy for a proper message."

"Okay, Thaina? Do you have anything?"

Thaina shook her head. "I'm good, sir. Weapons are online until they aren't. There's nothing to shoot right now though so I guess we're okay, huh?"

"For now," Kale agreed. "Okay, go ahead and get back to work."

Kale sat down and brought up what they knew about the new planet. The information was disappointingly light but Deva would offer more soon. The tech crews in their lab would be analyzing the data as well. If their equipment was capable of determining what they were looking at, they'd figure it out.

If not...well, Kale always wanted to explore the unknown.

Strange that I have the chance to be part of an expeditionary force in the middle of a war. I just wish it wasn't out of necessity.

Orbiting the planet might be risky. When they got closer, they'd be able to determine the viability of the process. Until then, they had quite a while to perform their work and prepare for what was to come. Kale worried about his crew but deep down, he thrilled at the situation they were in.

This is the type of situation that shows what kind of leader you really are and whether or not you're ready for the position. I look forward to proving it...and getting us all home at the end.

"Um…Anthar?" Deva spoke up. "I've got one more thing to report."

"Okay," Kale replied. "Go ahead."

"It's about the time…the fact that the date shows differently than we expected? Well…I've confirmed there's no data corruption." Deva sighed. "It's correct. We really have been gone for a very long time."

"Understood." Kale tried to remain calm but the notion deeply bothered him. Their friends and family would all consider them missing in action, lost in the conflict and possibly even dead. All those people had been put through one of the worse horrors imaginable: they had to wonder what happened to their loved ones.

I'll get us back now if I have to give my life. I swear it.

***

Siva waited at the space port for the Behemoth shuttle to arrive. Captain Gray Atwell and Clea An'Tufal were both on board and they had a lot to discuss before they could rush out and begin the search for The Crystal Font. Considering what they'd just come from, they probably needed some rest but there wasn't really time.

The folks lost out there needed help as soon as possible.

Guards stood nearby. They closed that particular wing of the port for privacy. That and Siva rarely ventured far away from her base. There she had complete control of the environment. Anywhere else and they had far too many variables to consider. Criminals, listening devices, bombs and other forms of violence were only a few and most of them could not be sufficiently accounted for.

I'm too close to success to risk my own life. I haven't picked a successor just yet.

The port authority nearly had a heart attack when her people took over. He couldn't do anything about it but he promised to make a formal complaint. Siva ensured his message went to one of her people working in the ministry, someone who would give it the attention it was due. Such small abuses of power felt petty but she didn't want to waste time explaining herself to high command. Not over something so small as a little civilian inconvenience.

That's the cost of security, folks.

Siva read through the limited information they already had concerning the whereabouts of the Crystal Font and hoped the Behemoth proved to be as good here as they did when the Orion's Light went after the monastery. The message came through clear enough but they were unable to relay reliable coordinates. Their intended destination might be a good place to start...but then she'd leave that up to the experts.

As the shuttle swept in and landed, she set aside her tablet and stood. Watching from the lounge, she sipped her drink and tried to remain patient. Maintenance people rushed out and secured the shuttle, the only people she wasn't absolutely certain about and as a result, each of them had a guard specifically assigned to watch them.

When did I become this paranoid? I'm in the capital! But that doesn't mean there aren't those who would cause trouble.

The ramp finally dropped and two Terran marines came down first, each armed. Her guests came down next, each in their dress uniforms. Gray's was white with several ribbons and the golden rank of Captain on his shoulder. Clea wore the severe kielan black with her own set of decorations showing off far more achievements than the humble woman's demeanor ever let on.

I like this girl. Mostly because I'm pretty sure she dislikes *me. She's definitely one of the good ones. I'm glad I've been keeping an eye on her.*

They were shown up to the lounge and Siva stepped forward as they entered, shaking their hands. "Welcome back! You both look well. Thank you for coming down here on such short and immediate notice. I appreciate it."

"Considering the news," Gray said, "you would've had to keep us away with a gun."

Siva adopted what she hoped looked like a sincere and concerned expression. It was one her mother used. Emotions became such a game to her, she only knew how to act them out. Day to day, she felt an abundance of duty more than anything else. As a result, it kept her from getting truly close to anyone.

"I'm very glad you both feel the same way I do. We need to get those men and women home."

Clea's brows raised. "Is that why we're doing this?"

Siva offered a thin smile. "The thing about assignments, tasks and missions is you can do them for any reason you want providing you get them done. Do it for the families, do it for the soldiers, do it for the military or me…but regardless of *why* we'll save that ship and bring it back here."

"Of course," Gray replied. "Are we meeting here?"

Siva nodded. "Yes, it's away from the base but we've vetted it. Plus, it'll be easier for you to get to high command from here when we're done. I'm sure they want to put you through the paces of a debriefing and all that. However, know that I've got you covered. You won't be there for more than an hour or two."

"Our ship needs to be resupplied," Gray said.

"Already underway. I believe someone contacted your executive officer the moment your shuttle departed and they're arranging everything you need. Plus, the data from that weapon you were hit with? We're analyzing it now. Extra medics are on the way to help your doctors scan everyone to ensure there were no lingering effects we have to worry about." Siva patted his shoulder. "I take care of my own, Captain."

"Thank you." Gray sat down. "I do appreciate the help. I would like to know why you want the Crystal Font back so badly that you've turned it into an intelligence matter. High command certainly would've sent ships to get them back, right?"

"Undoubtedly," Siva replied, gesturing to her glass. "Can I have them get you anything?"

"Water would be fine," Gray said. "So you were about to answer?"

"Okay, if you want me to keep things totally transparent." Siva leaned forward. "The Crystal Font just showed up out of nowhere. By the accounts of your log concerning that situation, it was more likely they were destroyed than missing. After all, you saw the flash and they were being pursued by a massive fleet. It stood to reason they all died. The *missing in action* report was put in to save the families some heart ache."

"Leaving them to wonder?" Gray asked. "When would they be deemed gone?"

Clea answered, "we have a regulation on the books stating that after one year without contact, a ship and its crew will be considered lost. All hands deceased."

Siva gestured to Clea. "There you have it. You do know your rules, Miss An'Tufal. Or should I say Tathin An'Tufal?"

"I'm not much for ceremony," Clea replied.

"Well, that's too bad because I got high command to go through the whole honor thing. They were going to march you before the council, read some poetry and have one of those cadets from secondary school pin the insignia on you." Siva sighed. "I suppose you'd rather not bother?"

"Er…are you serious?" Clea looked uneasy. Siva realized she still felt amusement, especially when poking at the overly intense officers she often encountered.

"No, not even remotely." Siva reached into her bag and tossed the young woman a box. "That's the insignia." She held up her tablet, showing Clea's official record. The rank increase already was applied. "And there you go. Officially on the registry and everything. Again, congratulations."

"Thank you." Clea opened the box but only looked in briefly. "I appreciate it."

"Bah." Siva waved her hand. "You and I both know your rank doesn't matter. You're not vying for the attention of promotion or trying to get into politics. You just want to do your job and do it well. I was like you so I get it. We're about the tasks, not the rewards. There's a reason we serve and it goes a lot deeper than money, pats on the back or prestige."

"You still haven't answered my question about why you want this ship back," Gray said.

"Ah, the Captain. Here to bring us back to reality." Siva tapped on her tablet. "The truth is I want that ship back here. I want to recruit Kale Ru'Xin into the ranks of intelligence and have them run ops for me. Provided they didn't survive on pure dumb luck, I can use resourcefulness like that. Like you have. There's a reason we're talking right now."

"I still don't know how you convinced my government of this," Gray said. "To put us to work I mean."

"It wasn't hard. Intergalactic cooperation for one." Siva shrugged. "And I can pull strings too. Your council doesn't quite know what to do with itself yet. Just entering into the arena of alien politics, they have to tread lightly and test the waters. Once they figure it out, I'm sure they'll have some demands. Every race joining the alliance does.

"Until that time, it leaves them vulnerable to people like me who are able to...shall we say guide them, in the direction I need." Siva paused for effect. "And that's where you two come in. I'm able to give Clea what she was promised and keep her on your ship. You're able to provide me with the military might I don't possess without these deals. Together, we get things done. How's that for transparent?"

"Pretty good," Gray said. "So what happens to us when we get the Font back?"

"I hope you'll stick around. I know you want a shot at the enemy's home world but we've got a lot to do between now and then." Siva lowered her voice. "I can give you an update on the deadlock our high command has found itself in regarding battle strategy. They're not sure how they want to proceed. And with all the extra leaders at the table...it's complicated."

"So you're saying the attack is delayed," Clea said.

"Stalled," Siva replied, "would be a better term. They'll figure it out and when they do, I promise my games will not hold you back. You'll be out there in the front lines if you really want to be...but I'm pretty sure even in that conflict there'll be a better way for you to serve. Another avenue to help the cause. After all, any ship can sit in line to be battered. Few have the experience you do in being where one least expects."

"Like with novalat," Gray said. "When we showed up to turn the tide and ended up fighting the Orion's Light."

"Do you think they won't catch wind of where all our ships are going and find a way to be a nuisance? Honestly, the thorn in my side that is Krilan Ar'Vax…" Siva shook her head. "But we're not here to talk about that somewhat distant future. We're chatting about saving a lot of lives today. People I know you feel close to. I've sent you my data. Now, I need you to be fabulous and find them."

"Any suggestion on where to start?" Gray asked. "I don't recall you having a lot to go on."

"I don't." Siva shrugged. She gestured at Clea. "But this woman here had a dream and brought us the coordinates of the enemy planet. I'm pretty sure she can do anything."

"Um…" Clea blushed, rubbing the back of her neck. "I wouldn't go that far. It was luck…little more."

"Skill." Siva corrected. "Don't forget it. I've watched your career for a while, Miss An'Tufal. Since before you joined the Behemoth and were operating as a tech officer. Someone showed me your scores and I barely believed them. I even had a covert investigation go into whether or not you cheated."

Clea's mouth dropped. "Excuse me?"

"It's true." Siva shrugged. "And when I learned you had not, I was all the more impressed. I put you on my watch list, so to speak. The good kind, by the way…not like Krilan or anything. I must admit I was pretty surprised when they sent you to be a liaison for the humans but it made sense in a way. Top of the class graduate would do more for them than a diplomat. After all, you had to teach them about the tech too, right?"

"They were fast learners," Clea muttered.

"Sure they were. And they had a fantastic teacher." Siva sipped her drink again. "In any event, I think we've done enough polishing of ego wouldn't you say? Captain, I'll let you get on with your day and we can meet again before you leave if you have any additional questions. However, I'm pretty sure you have everything and anything I can give. What do you think, Clea?"

"I…agree."

"We'll talk later then," Gray said. "Thanks for meeting us here."

"Best way to catch you right off the boat."
Siva shook his hand again. "Lovely to talk as
always. Good luck out there. I hope you won't
need it but these days, who knows, right?"

"Indeed." Gray opened the door. "Clea?"

"Um...if you don't mind," Siva said. "I'd like
a quick private word with Miss An'Tufal."

Gray's brows raised but he nodded once,
stepping out. Clea looked uneasy with the offer but
remained still. The two women observed one
another, remaining quiet. When finally Siva broke
the silence, she prefaced her words with a smile.
She needed to get this girl on her side, to make
her a friend even in pretense if necessary.

"I'm sure you don't appreciate my
methods," Siva said. "But I would like you to know
I do everything I do for the sake of the alliance.
Not merely kielans, but every race we've embraced
as our friends. I want the universe to be a safer
place."

"I know that, ma'am."

"Clea, what if I told you I wanted to bring
you fully into the intelligence fold? To make you an
officer reporting directly to me?"

"I would be surprised," Clea said. "I haven't
really done anything to warrant such trust."

"Haven't you? You turned in your own sister and I know you could've found a way around it." Siva shook her head. "Your work has been beyond the call of duty and I know for a fact you have a lot more to offer than merely working as a liaison. Even as part of the crew there, your job can be better. I want to give that to you."

"At what cost?" Clea asked. "I don't want to be like Trellan."

"No, I don't think you're a covert operative and I wouldn't wish it on you. You're fondness for the humans shows you need to socialize without restraint." Siva turned and looked at the shuttle. "I have to admit to you, I haven't seen many officers come along with the right attitude to get things done as you and I. Eventually, I have to retire…or if something happens to me."

"What're you suggesting?" Clea asked.

"You're an amazing code breaker, you put together pieces of puzzles that don't remotely look like they go together and you're smart to boot. You know when to take orders and when to break them. I have not found anyone even close to as qualified to take over for me and since I get to pick my own successor…"

"You want me to…"

"Be my second." Siva looked her in the eyes. "At first, still serving aboard the Behemoth. Gathering intel about the places you visit. Being prepared for the main event in this war but afterward, you need somewhere to be. And I can't imagine a better place than working with me. Being my eyes and ears out there until such time as you take over. It's how my predecessor did it and I'd like to think he picked wisely."

"I...don't know what to say." Clea looked down. "It's a generous offer...an incredible one."

"Once in a lifetime."

"Yes..." Clea sighed. "Can I...can I think about it?"

"Do." Siva nodded. "Come back with The Crystal Font and give me your decision. Really do some soul searching. I think you'd like the perks we have to offer."

Clea moved for the door. "I need to catch up with Captain Atwell but...I'll talk to you soon."

"Perfect." Siva sat back down. "Thanks for stopping by and good luck." She finished off her drink and hoped the seed she planted would take root. A woman like Clea thrived on challenge and what Siva offered represented one of the greatest.

She'd very likely say yes and if not, well...there were other ways to seduce a mark.

Chapter 3

Clea found it difficult to concentrate through the rest of her meetings. Siva's comments stuck with her and left her wondering sort of indistinctly. Did she want to be a spymaster? The thought never occurred to her before but then, who aspires to such a position? It seemed unlikely one could simply *decide* on the intelligence track.

Her friends who joined the overt version of the division didn't apply for it. They were offered the job after they finished their entrance exams, offered some oblique explanation for their eligibility. None of them even had the liberty to tell her where they trained or how long they'd be gone.

When they connected again, their conversations were guarded as if they didn't know how much to tell her about their personal lives anymore. She wondered whether their families experienced the same evasiveness. If so, Clea didn't want anything to do with it. Though after Vora, her sister, betrayed the alliance, she understood why people with classified info kept it to themselves.

Mother and father though? I guess filtering wouldn't be such a big deal.

Where does it stop though? A little omission here, an overt lie there...eventually, one might not even know the difference. Clea wondered if Siva even connected with her parents anymore. Kielans valued their families very much. Clea figured she might be able to ask her potential new boss some questions.

Should I ask Gray what to do? The thought of talking to the captain about her opportunity made sense. They'd spent a lot of time together over the past year but would it be okay? Should he know? Siva made the offer private after all and she made a point of it in fact. That was all the answer she needed.

This was one decision Clea had to make on her own. If she took the woman up on the offer, then none of her friends and family should know until there was a reason. The less they knew, the better in case...of what? Some random eventuality that involved an enemy? The idea made her sigh, a sound that drew a scowl from the superior officer in the meeting.

Someday, I might be in charge of your people, Clea thought. *So believe me, you prattling on about the budgetary concerns of the war effort aren't really that important to me right now. Especially since I have no influence over the people spending the money. Thanks, but I really should've just sat this one out.*

When Clea had time, she decided to visit the family estate well outside the city. During the early spring months, it tended to sit empty and she'd be able to really think, put some time to being alone. She needed to focus on the Crystal Font and how they were going to find them.

Gray told her they were going to spend two shifts in port before heading back out. Time might be of the essence and they needed to hurry if they hoped to save their friends. Clea knew that Olly and the rest of the tech crews would be absolutely invaluable in the process. They just needed to get out there.

And I have to shove aside my future for the time being. Kale and his people deserve my full attention. Especially after what they nearly sacrificed for us.

***

Kale felt immense pride in his crew for their efforts as they labored through the shift without rest. Their morale may have been shaken by what happened but they were bolstered by their escape from the enemy fleet. A sense of strength defied their worry. They felt like they could do anything. Fate truly felt on their side.

This didn't mean their obstacles were simple to overcome. As they moved toward the planet, preparations for replacing the crystal had the entire engineering team on edge. Repair crews throughout the ship continued to find minor systems that failed upon their jump recovery and the medical team was stretched beyond thin.

As Kale read through the various reports, he felt their exhaustion and sympathized. Unfortunately, he couldn't let up on them. All their lives depended on continuing on, finishing tasks and preparing for escape. They built in a rest schedule but few people actually wanted to leave their post.

The sense of ownership hit them all and no one wanted to be the weakest link in the chain that might eventually lead home. If the medical team hadn't been so tapped out, they would've certainly pushed for enforced rest cycles. Those already in the sick bay likely wouldn't be allowed to leave, ensuring at least half a shift worth of fresh faces in the event of an emergency.

Kale got to the quartermaster report and had mixed feelings. On one hand, they were well stocked for the next three weeks without rationing. Food supplies could be stretched to at least five weeks if necessary. They had far more severe problems but feeding the crew would matter pretty fast once they had to tighten their belts.

If the jump drive could not be repaired, they would be stranded for far longer than any amount of supplies could manage. They'd have to start foraging on any habitable worlds they could find, making a long trek to another system with a buoy that might bounce their communications far enough for someone to hear.

And even when they do hear, we'll have to hold out until they can send someone. They won't be able to drop everything and instantly hop out to us. We're going to have to hold out as long as we can. Maybe this planet will be our salvation. If it proves habitable, then we'll have no problem with resources as we wait for a rescue.

"Sir," Deva caught his attention. "We're near enough to the planet that I can get some better readings. I still have no idea what that energy is that we're reading but I'm able to scan the surface. Readings are all well within safety levels. Foliage, water and oxygen content are nearly ideal…which…well, that worries me."

"Yes, it does feel like quite the coincidence." Kale rubbed his chin. "Do you have any theories you'd like to share?"

Deva sighed. "Only a wild one. Our sensors have picked up some strange metallic content in the soil and rocks. The databases have nothing that match them compositionally. Combine that with the unknown energy and I'm curious if we've encountered a construct…a planet built by intelligent life."

Athan scoffed. "Impossible. No one has the technology to build something so large. And how would it be sustained? Their calculations would have to be miraculous to determine the exact distance from the star here."

Deva sat up straighter. "Interesting thought, Athan." She began tapping away at the console, her eyes narrow and focused. A few moments later, she grinned. "My theory has been given some weight. I believe this planet may have a variable orbit pattern, possibly modified by the energy reading."

"For what purpose?" Kale asked.

"Idealizing the atmosphere for whatever people are visiting," Deva said. "Why they would've made such a world, I can't say but if I'm right, then they've created a wonder. If we can study what they've done down there, then we would be able to forward our understanding of planetary reformation by generations."

"That's a bold statement," Athan said, "for something which I doubt is even remotely possible."

"Anything is possible," Deva said. "Your ten times great grandfather didn't believe moving faster than light would ever happen and here we are. Believe me, if someone can think a thing, it can become a reality. Don't get me wrong, if there's another explanation for what I'm seeing, I'll be excited to find it but right now, with the science we have available, I'm making some guesses."

"Fair enough." Kale closed his eyes in thought. "I want you to perform some additional scans. See if you can get an idea of how dangerous this place might be. Animals, sentient or otherwise, would be good. Poisonous foliage...anything you can pull. Also, we'll need to analyze the water and discover if there's anything edible."

"I'm on it, sir." Deva paused. "Gravitational pull seems unusually light. Far less than a body of that size *should* have. My calculations suggest we wouldn't even be able to achieve a traditional orbit because it wouldn't hold us."

Thaina huffed. "Seems like debris would've leveled this place by now based on everything you've figured out."

"I know," Deva replied. "The planet's energy emissions may also act as a repulsion beam. But how does it know what to keep away and what to allow close if I'm right? Honestly, I'm even guessing about that! We really need to go down there and learn more. This may be one of the greatest scientific discoveries of our culture."

Kale frowned at the screen, peering at the blue world they were approaching. The continents were clearly visible through light cloud coverage and vast seas made up a good part of the surface. His gut told him to be cautious, that they were walking into a dangerous situation. Before the additional facts came out, the place represented an oddity. Now, the unknown factors started stacking.

He didn't want to risk people unnecessarily.

"I need further analysis," Kale said. "I'm not comfortable sending anyone down there with that unknown power reading and where would we even land? These questions need answers before we go."

Deva didn't seem pleased. "I understand but many of the questions we're going to have will require onsite study. This place defies many of the conventions we take for granted. Wouldn't it be irresponsible to leave before we at least got a few answers?"

Kale replied, "our first order of business is keeping the crew alive and saving the ship. We can always come back to this place."

"I just..." Deva paused, biting her lip.

"Yes, I'm sure you want to be on the list of early discoverers. You have already catalogued more about this planet than anyone else." Kale stood up and approached her station, patting her shoulder. "And you have time to conduct further studies from up here. Until there's a reason, we're not heading down there though."

"Yes, sir." Deva still sounded disappointed but she returned to her duties. Kale understood her passion. He was curious as well but considering what they were up to and against, it seemed crazy to take risks. Especially when they were about to conduct one of the more difficult and complicated field repairs a starship could indulge.

I'd still like to know how the crystal broke. Kale had seen them fracture before during combat but the ship didn't take any fire on their way out. The drive wouldn't have worked otherwise. Still, they'd lost a lot of time and anything could've happened. They were all unconscious during their re-entry so no one knew just how rough it might've been.

Kale checked the computer logs but power was on minimum with pretty much all systems down. Their fate directly after the jump remained a mystery. He grunted, annoyed by the unknown all around them. Part of him wanted to have Deva start investigating the effects of the waste they dropped to escape, to see if their strange time loss might be repeatable.

Something told him it wouldn't be, that they were simply unlucky in that moment. Too many variables went on at the same time. Their velocity, the way the waste ignited, their proximity to a specific planet and all the debris floating about may well have created the perfect environment for their unplanned disappearance.

One thing helped. The enemy certainly couldn't have tracked them. And if they did, they never would've found them. A small favor but one that saved their lives. Kale considered his computer for a long moment, wondering if anyone had been through the system looking for them. Would the enemy have stopped at this strange world?

"Deva, have you been able to scan the surface for any crashed ships?" Kale asked. "Any tech that shouldn't be there?"

"The metal in the rocks and soil makes it a little hard to distinguish that," Deva replied, "but I'll check."

The thought might've been a long shot but nothing would've surprised him at that point.

A communication came through from the medical bay, a text message warning him he needed to take a rest period. *Ah, they must've caught up if they can start worrying about that now.* He was exhausted and agreed with them but there were several things that needed to happen before he could turn over temporary command.

He reached out to Meira. "How're you doing on preparations for the crystal swap?"

"We've got the new one prepped and we've nearly finished the risk analysis. I'll be filing my report in an hour but I have to be honest, I'd rather not do this before my people can get some downtime. Believe me, we want everyone alert and hardy for this procedure. Any mistakes can strand us here for a *very* long time."

"Understood." Kale rubbed his eyes. "Okay, finish the analysis and pack it in for a shift. When you're all back, fed and rested, revisit what you did and see if you missed anything. We'll reconvene mid fourth shift."

"Yes, sir. Thank you."

The line closed and he turned to Athan. "How're you doing?"

"I'm fine, sir. A little tired but nothing I can't live with."

"I'm going to turn over temporary command to you while I take a rest period. Let's not make any rash decisions while I'm gone. Business as usual. Wake me for any emergencies but otherwise, we remain close but not too close to the planet. Deva, finish up what you're doing and head to your quarters as well. We'll take turns until everyone's refreshed."

Kale stood and felt his back complain. He hadn't been up long but waking from the strange event left him feeling as if he'd been through hard labor or a severe illness. He waited until he boarded the elevator before he stretched and rested against the wall.

The thought of sleep overwhelmed all his worries and he felt thankful for the fact. If his mind didn't let him turn off for a while, he'd be in for a long set of shifts. Considering what he'd been through, he'd likely call one of the doctors for a sedative. Much as he didn't want to drug himself, being exhausted wouldn't be much better.

***

Trellan En'Dal found himself in a difficult position. This wasn't unusual for him considering recent events but frustration gnawed at him regardless. After escaping the doomed Orion's Light vessel, he found himself on one of the novalat moon colonies carrying stolen plans for a new weapon. Something the authorities would do anything to get back.

Considering all he'd been through to make contact with the terrorist group, he could not be caught. Even landing proved to be a difficulty, avoiding scanner contact and evading notice by the military presence. Fortunately, the conclusion to a civil war kept them all busy so he managed to land his escape pod on the outskirts of an inhabited territory.

Though the moon orbited one of the larger planets, it was big enough to have its own breathable atmosphere. Trellan disembarked and made his way into town, keeping a low profile as he sought a way to escape the place. He needed a ship, or at least passage out of the system and he had nothing to trade.

All his personal items had been lost on the ship that exploded, including his weapons. Now, in a gray jump suit with a wrist computer and stolen property, he had to pull off the impossible. Leave the moon without attracting enough attention to get him chased or caught. Then, he'd be back to the *next* impossible mission: making a second contact with Orion's Light.

I must not like anything to be easy on a spiritual level. There's no other explanation for my luck.

Arriving at the space port was easy. He traveled along with every other person on their way to work. However, once he arrived, he observed how tight security had become. They may not have been watching the skies carefully but on the ground, their people were watch dogs. Every civilian had to provide identification and a biometric scan.

Two things Trellan lacked.

How am I going to get any of that in short order? I can't even steal a ship without getting through the first layer of security. Even if I do get in, there's bound to be additional check points. How do I keep things subtle while still getting in there?

A niggling thought tickled the back of his mind. He could always call out who he was and gain their cooperation. If they found out he worked for alliance intelligence, they'd be obliged to give him what he needed and get him on his way. But he couldn't risk it. They had no idea how deep the Orion's Light talons dug and if some informant put word out about him, the entire op, not to mention his life, would be in jeopardy.

No, I have to approach this problem like a criminal and run with it until I have no other options.

Trellan looked himself over and wondered what he must look like. The jump suit gave him a mechanic vibe but he didn't have any tools to pull off the look convincingly. If he wanted to mug someone for their cash or goods, he'd have to do it with his bare hands, which meant beating someone. A civilian didn't deserve that which left the guards.

They don't deserve it either. Taking them out might not be hard but even if I do, what sort of trouble will the poor bastard be in? I already screwed up some of their boys back on the planet. How many more do I have to sacrifice for this assignment?

The answer came to him quickly. *More*. He didn't like it, but the truth was if he wanted to leave, he'd have to turn to some level of violence, even if it involved hurting an innocent. Orion's Light represented a threat to the entire galaxy. Knocking someone out would pale in comparison to what inaction might accomplish.

Okay, so who? And where? I don't know this place so dumping an unconscious body won't be easy. Maybe a distraction's a better way to go but the louder I get, the more people I'll put in harm's way.

Trellan sat in a public area and forced himself to look casual. Resting felt good. He hadn't been able to take any real downtime for several shifts. Even with the stress of what he had on him, he was able to let his muscles loosen up and take a deep breath while evaluating his situation.

The most important thing to remember was they were not actively looking for him. This meant any police or soldiers shouldn't pay him any mind. The foot traffic of every day civilians was dense enough to let him blend in. No one could remember every face and all the cameras were closer to the port entrance.

A legal route off the planet is not an option. Escaping with his stolen plans would be impossible if he tried to go through security the proper way. They'd search him, both electronically and physically. Even if they didn't know what they had by sight, their scanners would show what he had.

Local ports had a habit of checking for stolen data since so many people tried to smuggle it around. Trellan didn't have time to work with a computer to obfuscate it so he was stuck with a live drive that would immediately tell any computer operator that he was carrying stolen goods. He was back to the illegal route.

Not only did he need to get past security, but he required a ship that was jump capable. If he fled the moon in anything else, they'd catch him in no time. If he got through and launched without clearance, he'd need to plot a course and be away in less than twenty minutes. Anything longer and he'd be facing their military.

Distracted or not, they'd definitely make time to catch a pirate making off with something so expensive. And it would be compounded if they suspected he carried those plans.

After an hour, he left the area for fear of being suspicious for loitering. His stomach growled and he desperately wanted a little sleep. Unfortunately, neither requirement would be easy to fulfill considering his situation. He found himself wandering down a side street near a couple of restaurants when he saw a security officer stumble out of a bar.

That might just work...at least to get me inside.

The man leaned against a wall, struggling to maintain his footing. Trellan moved closer and looked around, noting they weren't quite alone but the population was a lot thinner in that part of town. Apparently, whatever shift was happening there didn't afford a lot of patrons for the shops.

A security guy might have an easier time slipping in. Providing they don't all know each other but I'm going to take a chance here. There are enough people roaming around for there to be far too many authority figures to keep track of. Sorry, guy. I have to get out of here.

Trellan stepped closer to the man and gently took him by the arm. The security guard looked at him with a startled expression but didn't try to pull away. "I didn't do nothin' in there," he slurred. "What...what do you want?"

"Come with me, sir." Trellan urged him toward the alley. "We need to talk."

"What for? I already said I didn't do anything. Leave me alone. I just need to get back to the barracks."

"In a minute." Trellan used more force and the man stumbled after him. They paced half way down the alley to the darkest part. The guard constantly muttered the whole way, mostly gibberish. If he was nervous, he did a fantastic job of hiding it but the booze must've fortified him. When they reached a dumpster, they stopped.

"Oh boy…you're not going to hit me, are you?"

Trellan frowned. "Afraid so. You'll be fine in a couple hours, buddy." He drew back and clocked the man square in the jaw, the force of the blow knocking the inebriated man out immediately. As he began to collapse, Trellan caught him and propped him up against the trash and stripped him of his uniform.

The whole process took several minutes and every second made Trellan more and more nervous. He knew that anyone who happened to glimpse down on them would see what was going on and the whole plan would be ruined. There were few places to go beyond the settled part of the moon and without knowledge of the area, he'd get lost fast.

Why do these guys have so many buttons on their shirts? Seriously, this fashion is ridiculous!

Trellan tore off his own jump suit and forced himself to calm down, pulling on the garments slowly. He didn't want to rip anything or the whole exercise would be wasted. The man's boots were too small but the rest fit reasonably well. He hoisted the naked guard and deposited him in the dumpster, strapped on the guy's firearm and steadied himself for the dangerous part of his plan.

Security guards themselves may have been searched as well when they entered the facility but he hadn't noticed any during his hour long observation. Chances were good they had a side door, one he might slip through and into the port proper. Whatever came after would be a mystery he'd have to address on the fly.

The planning phase ended, especially since it was only a matter of time before the man he assaulted woke up and raised an alarm.

Trellan rushed back to the courtyard and slowed down as he came in contact with other people. Blending in, he walked confidently beside them and noticed he was given a wide berth. Luckily, the uniforms didn't have any name tags on them but they were pretty obvious in their light gray with black piping. The firearm also contributed to the overall look.

Unfortunately, Trellan hadn't shaved in days but at least his beard was filled in enough to look intentional. Three days earlier he wouldn't have been able to pull off his disguise in the slightest. Approaching the stairs, he cast his gaze around for a sign indicating which direction he was expected to take as staff.

Panic gripped his heart as he drew closer until he caught the thing he was looking for. Security on duty were directed to go around to the left. A security card would be required but it didn't look like anyone got searched. All the better. He drew out the man's ID and swiped it, causing the door to buzz before it swung open. He paced through as if he belonged and continued down a hallway.

No one was around but he figured a camera picked up his entrance. They might be running facial recognition so once again, he felt the crunch of time. The schedule gripping his chest made him nervous but he forced himself to remain calm, taking regular breaths and walking without urgency.

A guard started approaching from in front of him and Trellan wondered if he might need to defend himself. The guy nodded to him as they passed one another, barely taking heed. As he reached the second door leading into the port, he didn't hesitate, opening up and stepping inside.

People milled about, carrying out business as usual. Trellan watched for a brief moment, trying to decide how best to get himself onboard a ship and out of there. He needed a computer, one that he could access for several moments without interruption. They'd have a manifest of all visitors and whether or not they were interstellar crafts.

A nearby public terminal looked like it would do the trick with only a little coaxing. Trellan approached casually and tapped the screen, bringing up a couple of options. One was for visitors and another offered access for security or maintenance personnel. He tapped security and was forced to swipe his card.

A screen appeared, letting him know it was accessing the required information. he glanced around, noting that no one seemed to be paying attention to him. The terminal beeped once, indicating it had information ready for him. Menu items offered security footage as well as lists for visitors and currently docked ships.

He tapped the silhouette of space vessels and held his breath, suddenly aware that there may not *be* any interstellar visitors. Luckily, there was and it didn't look like it would be too difficult to pilot alone. It was at docking bay sixteen, not too far from his current location but due to leave in two hours.

The owners might be there. The thought of robbing some people of their property, especially something so big as a ship, made his stomach knot. He had to get it done but they'd be stranded, inconvenienced at best with a worst case scenario involving bankruptcy. He might be able to get the government to help them out after he left.

He'd have the ability to send messages again and catch up with Siva. Maybe they'd have another plan to deal with Orion's Light and he'd be able to go home. Trellan wouldn't let that hope blossom but it sat in the back of his mind, taunting him with the possibility. Stranger things had happened.

Someone behind him cleared their throat and he looked to see a well dressed businessman tapping his foot. "You going to be on there all day?"

"Performing some maintenance," Trellan replied. "I'm all done." He cleared the terminal and stepped away. "There you go."

"About time." The man muttered, going about his business.

Trellan moved toward the hallway leading to the docking bay, arriving at the door when he heard someone shout. He ignored it, not even bothering to look but he did pick up the pace just a little, allowing urgency to compel him. Another cry, this time more insistent, made him glance. Someone was waving in his direction.

What do they want? Trellan waved back and they nodded, gesturing for him to come back. He ignored the command and opened the door, stepping through and closing it behind him. Engaging the locking mechanism, he noted the cameras in his peripheral vision. *Time to really move, I guess.*

Trellan picked up the pace, jogging down the hall while reading signs. Various doors led off to different bays and he had to go nearly to the end to reach sixteen. He was half way there when the door he came in through opened up and several people came spilling in. He shifted to a sprint.

"You there!" Someone shouted. "Stop! What're you doing?"

How'd they figure it out? Trellan's mind spun up, trying to think of what might've given him away. Had the guard woken up? Did their facial recognition kick in? Did he step out of place? It didn't ultimately matter. He'd been caught. Getting out of there might be a miracle, one he knew he had to create himself.

The map he pulled up indicated he was getting closer to the ship. Tech crews should've been done prepping it for launch. They were just waiting for their window to depart and the crew, however many of them there might be, would either be on board or nearby. That meant he'd have to come on pretty strong.

Trellan burst through a door into the open air, the ship sitting less than a hundred yards away with the sky above them. *I'm really damn close!* People looked startled as he came in and he decided to play up his costume for all it was worth. "I'm with station security. We've got a fugitive on the run. You see anyone come in here recently?"

He counted five people total, two women and three men. They were near the ramp to the ship and could easily board. If they were able to do so before he got close, they'd lock it up and he'd be done. If Trellan could distract them long enough for him to get close, he'd get out of there. Otherwise, the guards would overtake him.

"Just you," the largest of the men spoke up, taking a step forward to greet him. "We just got an alert on the com about something going on."

"It's pretty bad," Trellan said, trying to buy time as he continued walking. He knew the closer he'd get the more obvious it would become he was out of place. Covered in sweat, exhausted and unkempt, he his disguise was only meant to confuse enough for him to get into the place and find a way out. "Have you heard any racket?"

"Should we board the ship?" One of the women asked. "Maybe we can lock ourselves down until the situation is resolved."

"Not a bad idea," Trellan said. "But have you all been here the whole time? Has someone always been watching the ramp? Our suspect may have boarded when you weren't looking."

"Unlikely," the big guy replied. "Look, I'm going to need to see some ID."

Just then, the door behind them burst open and the real security personnel came in. "Get away from that man!" The lead soldier barked, pointing in their direction. Trellan was only a few paces from the civilian. He dashed forward and grabbed the man by the wrist while drawing his weapon.

Placing it to the side of his hostage's head, Trellan started moving toward the ship again. "Drop your weapons or I'll shoot him."

"Put your gun down!" Station security ordered. "We won't tell you again. This is going to get bad if you don't comply."

"Already looks pretty bad," Trellan said. "Now, I need the civilians to step away from the ship or I'll start shooting people. Believe me, this is not the sort of disaster you want on your hands. If I hurt a bunch of innocents because you don't comply, then what's your superior going to say? How do you think you'll answer the hard questions?"

"I can't let you take that ship."

"Take our ship?" The other woman spoke up. "Are you kidding? Shoot him already!"

"Lira!" Trellan's hostage cried out. "Have you noticed I'm right here?"

Trellan glanced over his shoulder and noted he was within twenty yards of the ramp. Luckily, the spacers were too stunned to take any action. They could've locked the thing down and he'd be dead in the water. Instead, they gawked at the spectacle, buying him a little more time to make his miracle.

"Listen," Trellan muttered to the man he was holding. "I'm very sorry about this. Believe me, if there were another way, I wouldn't be doing this...but I have to leave this place."

"Just settle down, sir," the hostage kept his hands raised as he spoke. "Please, we didn't do anything to you. You should surrender to the security people. They'll shoot you otherwise!"

"Put the gun down!" Security shouted again. "We are *not* going to keep warning you!"

"But you're not going to shoot me either," Trellan replied. "Not with the hostage in the way. Back off or he dies."

"Whoa!" Trellan's hostage cried out. "Come on, I don't deserve this!"

"No, you don't," Trellan said. "Believe me, I know." He approached the ramp and the sense of desperation increased in the security people. They knew the moment he boarded the vessel, he'd be difficult to dislodge and if he launched, they'd have to turn over his capture to someone else.

The rest of the crew tried to bar his way, standing in front of the ramp. "We're not letting you on our ship!" The one called Lira spoke. "Give up already! This is ridiculous!"

"I'm going to shoot this guy in the head," Trellan said. "And maybe I'll get shot shortly after but I'll tell you what, the next person who dies is you, Lira." The comment made her gasp. "Yeah, I'm sure you're not used to people telling you like it is but there you go. You *will* be the second person to go even if I'm next. Now back off!"

Someone pulled her aside and they gave him space to go up the ramp.

"What're you doing?" Security shouted. "Stop him!"

"That's your job!" Lira yelled back. "Don't let him get away!"

Trellan backed up the ramp, pulling his hostage with him. "I doubt you want to come with me," he said. "When we get to the top, you've got five seconds to get back down there. Understand?"

"Please, you can't take our ship. This is our home, our livelihood! Sincerely…we'll take you where you want to go, I swear it."

"You and I both know you're not able to be honest in this situation." Security came close enough to see so Trellan took two shots, driving them back. He saw the panel to close the door. "Okay, get going. This is your last chance. Start shouting at them not to shoot or they might get trigger happy. Go!"

"But…please!"

"I said go!" Trellan booted the man in the rump, propelling him forward. The poor bastard stumbled and nearly fell, shouting as loud as he could for them to not fire at him. Someone grabbed him and dragged him out of the way, firing into the ship just as Trellan hit the button to seal it.

As the ramp went up, the shouts of his pursuers became muffled. He rushed to the cockpit and checked the controls, thanking the fates that they were getting ready to leave. The engine was primed and ready for take off. He kicked on the shields and engaged the thrusters, lifting off.

The radio lit up from tower control, demanding to know what he was doing. Trellan ignored it, directing the vessel at an angle before departing. He felt tempted to hit the burners for a swifter getaway but he knew the people down there might get incinerated in the process. They were likely already uncomfortable and he'd done enough damage for one day.

The moment he cleared the area though, he kicked the burners on and broke atmosphere in a few seconds. Ships hailed him, demanding answers to his swift departure. It wouldn't take them long to figure out he'd stolen the ship and wasn't simply a defiant spacer wanting to get moving.

Trellan plotted a course for an out of the way system where he could provide an update to intelligence. From there, he'd be able to hop over to one of the old pirate hangouts and take some downtime while trying to find the Orion's Light again. He had to fight frustration about starting over from scratch, especially when he'd been so close.

Fighters on his radar cast aside concerns as he focused on evasion. The navigation computer didn't want him to go to his destination, warning it was in the middle of nowhere. He had to initiate an override, which took almost a full minute. Plenty of time for fighters to get close enough to engage.

As they drew nearer, he picked up the com, hoping to buy some time.

"Star Skimmer, this is the Novalat Police," the voice crackled in his ear. "You are instructed to power down your engine and surrender immediately or we will blow you out of the sky."

"You'd rather destroy the ship than give it back to its owners, huh?" Trellan asked. "Seems a little wasteful to me, don't you think? What guarantees do I get if I surrender? How will I be treated?"

"That shouldn't really matter to you right now since you're facing death," came the reply. "Power down immediately. We will not give you a third warning."

"I'd like to negotiate." Trellan looked at the course and he had less than twenty seconds. "Will you feed me? I had to steal the ship because I'm starving."

"That's it." Pulse blasts flew past the ship and he initiated an array of evasion maneuvers, doing his best to keep ahead of them. Unfortunately, the merchant ship wasn't meant for combat and he was lucky to keep it flying straight let alone avoiding incoming attacks.

The shields flared twice and he knew he wouldn't get a third. The computer chimed, letting him know it was ready. Slapping the panel, he engaged the jump drive and held his breath. *I hope you people had decent equipment*. The shouts of the security people rang over the com as he winked out.

Trellan escaped.

Chapter 4

Two hours into their trip toward the planet, Kale received an update from the engineering team. They would be ready to make the transition for their crystal at the beginning of the next shift, nearly three and a half hours away. Right around the same time, they'd arrive at the mysterious planet and have some options in the event the jump drive was too severely damaged.

Kale had Wena engage a ship wide com, leaning toward the mic to address the crew. He'd been rehearsing some of what he intended to say since he promised Eirkan he'd talk to them all. As he opened his mouth to speak, most of the prepared speech disappeared and he had to improvise.

"This is Anthar Ru'Xin. I know you've all been operating with little information about our current situation. I'd like to offer you some now. First, our departure from the research facility proved to be both a success and a failure. The ploy to use waste from the pulse drive damaged our jump capability. We are currently stranded in this section of space.

"Before you begin to worry, however, please note that engineering is working on repairing the damage. They will begin the process in around four hours. Until then, we are speeding toward a planet in this system which appears to be habitable. A buoy is orbiting the world and we plan to ensure it is online to send a request for help.

"As we approach our problem from multiple angles, I need you all to stay focused on your tasks and do the best job you can do. We've come this far together and I fully intend to get you home. Please direct any questions to your section heads. I'll be hosting a briefing for them shortly. Thank you."

Athan glanced over his shoulder, "well done, sir."

"Thank you," Kale replied with a smirk. "I'm glad you approve. Deva, do you have anything to report?"

"Not really, sir. I believe when we arrive, I'll be able to pull a lot more data from the planet. Engineering has repaired all minor damage throughout the ship. There are no more outstanding work orders for assistance at this time. Medical reports people are returning to their posts or quarters. All in all, if not for the jump drive we'd be at near one hundred percent."

Kale nodded and returned to his own computer, reading through the reports she mentioned. As he finished, he turned his attention to the view screen and the planet ahead of them. He wanted to know more but as they approached, he knew in the back of his mind he would not be sending anyone down there. The risk was too great.

And without the support of the alliance behind him, he wasn't taking any unnecessary chances. It would probably break Deva's heart but maybe she could be part of the next visit they made. Until then though, their sole focus *had* to be getting the jump drive back and fixing the buoy. Their lives depended on one or the other.

His eyes began to burn and he realized he needed to take the advice of the medical team. Even if it was a short nap. Still, he didn't have time. The briefing he promised would probably eat up a third of the shift. Then they'd be switching out the crystal and he couldn't be sleeping then.

Looks like I'll be taking a couple stimulants after all. The thought didn't make Kale happy. While they certainly kept him awake, they'd always left him with head aches in the past. Today would likely be no different. He leaned back in his chair and tried not to relax too much. On his way to meet the section heads, he'd visit medical.

***

Fully outfitted and ready to go, the Behemoth made their departure from port, heading toward deep space for a jump. They didn't have a destination as of yet, but Clea, Olly and Paul Baily were working on it. As they congregated in one of the tech labs, their computers ran through dozens of options for where the Crystal Font might've jumped to.

"The problem," Clea began, "is that they could've made multiple jumps by now. However, an emergency hop tends to only be a system away...like a slightly longer micro jump. We *could* start in those systems nearby and look for any sign of them. Chances are good such signatures have dissipated though."

Olly hummed. "What if we went to a central location?" He brought up a star map and pointed at a system adjacent to the research facility. "If we go here, we can systematically grab data from all the buoys. If the enemy didn't take theirs out, it might even have course data."

Clea shook her head. "It won't. Standard procedure when fleeing an engagement is ensuring no data is transmitted. Otherwise, the enemy could've just followed them and considering they thought they had the research we were trying to protect, I guarantee they would've."

"Fair point...but at least we'd get the buoy data from other points."

Paul spoke up. "I've got a question. When the Crystal Font left the system, we thought they exploded. I read the report. Now we know they didn't so what could've caused that impression? What could they have done to make us think they blew up?"

Clea smiled, grateful for the young man's insight. "Good question, Mister Baily. There are several things that come to mind. They likely wanted to buy themselves some space. They could've jettisoned explosive cargo...bomb ordinance for example."

"What else makes such a spectacular explosion?" Olly asked. "I think detonating one of our pulse bombs so close to the ship would be too risky. They're designed to take out installations and would easily chew through shields. Lord knows the enemy was hammering them too. It would've practically been suicide."

"I'm running a simulation," Paul said. "Typically, we recycle pulse waste but it takes a while for the stuff to be usable. It's pretty volatile for several days. Could they have used that to make their escape? Dumped a whole bunch and jumped out on that? Would've definitely distracted the enemy."

Clea felt skeptical but couldn't outright deny the idea. "It seems unlikely only because no one could predict what the stuff would do. It could interfere with coordinates and that's the most subtle problem. Still, if they did that there may *still* be traces today after all this time. Of course, we'd have to use long range scans to do any of the work."

"Because the enemy might still be there," Olly said.

Clea nodded. "An adjacent system would give us an opportunity to get the most detailed scan possible. However, confirming they did something crazy doesn't necessarily get us closer to finding them." She brought up the communication Siva shared with them. "This came through the main buoy of our home world. Let's tap into the network and see what we can come up with."

They put their heads down for some time, each attacking the problem from a different angle. Clea knew they needed to get something from the buoy before they reached their destination. Gray would expect a destination when they were in a position to jump. But the vastness of space made the prospect intimidating.

Hundreds of thousands of messages went through the various buoys on a daily basis. The cache was dumped every hour and a half. The good news was Siva's people made a backup of all the activity in the time immediately before and for thirty minutes after The Crystal Font's message came in. Clea brought up the data and looked at time stamps.

Everything followed a strict sequence, being routed and delivered by a triply redundant software package. They were broken up into multiple categories. In system messages came from no farther than the space station on the border near the furthest planet out. Out of system messages could come from anywhere but they did have a range limit.

Clea wasn't sure what specific parameter was used but a third category came from *distant* places. These were messages that likely had to bounce from buoy to buoy to make it back to the planet. They could be only a few days old or pushing months. Her heart hammered as she checked the backup logs.

This has what buoy the message came from. Clea checked but her shoulder slumped. The last buoy the message touched was an adjacent system where several colony worlds operated. If the Crystal Font was there, they would've already received help. Furthermore, they couldn't follow the message because the buoy may well have already purged the message.

Still, there's a chance there. Even if the message has been deleted, we know it came from that place. "Olly," Clea said, "bring up all buoys adjacent to this one...here." She tapped her tablet and brought up the system over's buoy. "Show me the network from that point spanning outward.

"I'm on it but..." Olly paused to work. "I'm not sure how it's going to help. These messages could've come from *anywhere*. How can we narrow down the one they came from?"

"Oh!" Paul spoke up. "Check it out. There has to be buoys that don't get as much traffic. Those might not have purged the data yet. Right?"

"A distinct possibility," Clea said. "Definitely an option for us to check. We also know they aren't in a high traffic area or else they would've already received help. Finally, they must be in some system with a buoy to have sent that message at all. They may have been there this whole time stuck too...and it could've taken so long for their initial message to reach us."

"I just wish they had been able to say more," Paul said. "Like some coordinates would've been nice."

"Too easy," Olly replied. "Anyway, we've got this."

Durant Vi'Puren stepped into the room, carrying his tablet. His white lab coat fluttered around him as he took a seat at the head of the table and launched into an update without so much as acknowledging them. "I've done some analysis of the message we received from the Font. The interference should help us locate them."

"How so?" Clea asked.

"Initially, I thought the static was simply degraded quality, bits lost in the digital transfer.

But when I took a closer look, I found that I could clean up the message sufficiently to remove all the potential noise. When I isolated that, I discovered a steady, rhythmic wave...some kind of energy reading." Durant grinned. "And my favorite part is I have no idea what could generate it."

"Is that good?" Olly's brows lifted. "I mean, if *you* don't know what it is...that sounds bad."

"It'll be fascinating and we'll definitely learn something on this trip," Durant replied. "Anyway, I had the computer compare it to every form of engine and machinery in our database but nothing came close to matching. It truly is a mystery."

"How will that help us find them?" Paul asked.

Durant hummed. "Through the process of elimination. We can rule out systems that do not have the energy reading."

"How far out can we get that information?" Clea asked. "Because we don't want to go hopping all over creation."

"I'm not sure, I'm still writing a program to detect it." Durant shrugged. "But for now, what've you come up with?"

"We're checking the buoy network," Olly said. "I've finished mapping it out and we can take a look now."

Clea tapped the received link and watched the network form outward from the home world, reaching far and wide. Olly marked all the buoys that were in remote systems and the number was much higher than she hoped. Her vision was they might have a dozen or so but as she watched the numbers climb, she realized they'd have a hard time collecting from even half of them.

They needed a way to limit their searches, to narrow the parameters. Clea decided to assume they only jumped once until they had evidence to the contrary. The idea that they hopped out then found another system to go to seemed unlikely and if they did, they might be flat out impossible to find without another message.

Taking a look at the research area, she noted that the buoy there was still active. Also, it was off the civilian grid. Only their military software even located it. She squinted at the screen and filtered by the least used buoys in the area. Seven began to blink. Three were in close proximity to the compromised research facility.

"These buoys are interesting," Clea said. "They barely have any use, especially since the research facility fell to the enemy."

"Didn't the military shut that off?" Durant asked. "If not, they should've. Anyone in close proximity could hack into it...learn our coding methods."

"No," Clea replied. "They just take it off the standard routing. By leaving it on, we retain a valuable tool. For example, if we wanted to spread some disinformation, we could turn it back on a few days early, route some gibberish through it then send the falsehood. Our enemies would pick it up and have to second guess whether or not we were telling the truth."

"Ah..." Durant nodded. "This is why I'm not in the military I suppose."

"In any event, we can use it to determine if the enemy is still in that section of space but, we have to be closer." Clea rubbed her chin. "At least one system away...at one of the adjacent buoys so we can connect up to it and send the activation code. We can observe the research system and get scan information to determine how The Crystal Font actually left the area."

"You think there's anything left to scan?" Paul asked. "It seems like it would've dissipated by now."

Olly added, "not to mention the fact we had a pretty big engagement there. I'm guessing any debris will interfere with our scans, especially with something as rudimentary as the buoy."

"We can get all we need," Clea replied. "And if they did what we think, then the signature will not have dissipated. That waste material, even ignited, stays around for a long time. It takes a while to recycle for a reason."

"So you recommend we go to one of these three adjacent buoys," Durant said, "scan it for information then check the compromised system to determine our next move?"

Clea nodded. "Exactly."

"Sounds reasonable," Paul said. "I can get behind it."

"Me too," Olly added.

"I'll talk to the captain," Clea said. "You'll want to get back to your posts. When we arrive, we're going to have to be on alert. This is dangerous territory we're about to enter and if we have to fight, you should be ready."

***

Kale woke as his computer chimed, indicating he had a communication. He checked, noting the caller as Meira. He sat up, rubbed his eyes and tapped the button, doing his best to sounded awake and refreshed. The way his voice cracked, he failed miserably but couldn't muster too much concern, at least in that moment.

"Anthar Ru'Xin here."

"Anthar," Meira began, "I'm sorry to have woken you. We...have a bit of a problem."

"I'll be down in a moment." Kale killed the connection and washed his face, drying it quickly before throwing his uniform back on. Checking himself in the mirror, he knew he had to continue to look his best despite the circumstances. The crew needed to see him as dauntless if their morale was to remain positive.

He headed down to the engineering section and paced inside, looking around for anything overtly out of place. People continued to work, moving about the area between panels, taking care of different tasks. He found Meira by the crystal assembly chamber with several other technicians gathered around. She broke away and joined him.

"The crystal's ready to put in," Meira said. "But I've performed several tests and I'm afraid we have to spark it. Something happened in the jump and the container became unsealed."

Kale knew the term well. It essentially meant they needed to give the gem enough juice to power the jump drive, a procedure typically performed in port. The last time it was done on a ship he worked on, he'd been a pilot. He remembered the stress around the situation then though the gravity of it then wasn't what it was now.

If they didn't find a way out there, they'd be stranded.

"I understand." Kale scratched the back of his neck. "Do you have a plan? Any thoughts on how we might go about it?"

"All our generators combined can't generate that kind of power," Meira said. "But I spoke with Deva and she believes the energy on the nearby planet could work. I ran some simulations and I have to agree with her. There's plenty down there. We just have to figure out how to harness it and pump it into the crystal."

"There are a lot of *ifs* in that plan," Kale pointed out. "Not to mention the fact we might not be able to survive on the surface of that planet. None of us has any clue what we're getting into down there."

"The risks are outweighed by the potential benefits," Meira said. "If we don't try, there's nothing we can do up here to spark this."

"What about using the other crystal?"

"The moment it leaves the assembly, it's going to drain fast. The cracks are bad. It'll be useless in less than ten minutes. The only reason it hasn't given out already is the chamber it's in...storing that power to ensure it doesn't simply dissipate."

Kale nodded. "I understand...it does sound like the planet might be our only hope. Unfortunately."

"I'm afraid so. But Deva has done some outstanding work cataloging the place. She knows a great deal about the energy field, the foliage, the surface and the water. And I can spare a tech crew to help find a way to harness that power."

Kale smirked. "I would hope so considering the situation."

Meira shook her head. "A standard response for a nonstandard situation. But in any event, how long before we send someone down?"

"When will you put the new crystal into the assembly?"

"When we have a method to spark it," Meira replied. "The generators can't keep us going for long. At least we're operating right now."

"Understood." Kale looked at the broken crystal, considering the situation for a long moment in silence. Several things needed to happen before he felt comfortable having anyone set foot on that world. The first of which involved recon outside of Deva's scans. He turned to Meira and patted her arm. "Thank you for the assessment. I'll contact you when we're ready."

"We're poised and ready to take care of it the moment we can," Meira said. "Good luck, sir."

Kale headed to the bridge, feeling pressured by fate. Deva was probably right. They needed to know what was happening down there and how the planet came to be. Their investigation for the power source would likely gather other answers as well. So far, the place seemed rather accommodating.

Now to find out if that's actually true.

Kale stepped off the elevator into the bridge and immediately approached Deva. "It seems you'll get your wish. We're going to have to go down to the planet."

"Sir?" Deva's eyes widened. "But you said..."

"I know," Kale interrupted. "We've got a problem with the replacement crystal. It needs to be sparked." His comment led to several groans throughout the ship. "I know. But Meira has a plan and it involves using the energy source on the planet below. We just have to go down there to determine how we can harness it. Deva, have you found any dangerous plants or animals?"

"No, sir." Deva shook her head. "But honestly, as I mentioned before, it's hard to get too fine of detail due to the metal in the rocks and soil. I will say this, it is unlikely we would be able to grow food down there. It would have to be done in green houses with heavily filtered dirt. At least, that's my assessment."

"Let's hope we don't have to start a farm," Athan muttered.

"Thank you for the commentary," Kale said, returning his attention to Deva. "We're going to launch several fighters to scout the area. I want you to coordinate their efforts and tap into their scanners. They'll be able to get closer which should help I assume. Get them to narrow down where we should go to find the power source. It's a big planet and we don't want to wander too much."

"Yes, sir."

"Athan, get us a little closer. Just on the verge of their gravitational field."

"That's practically right on top of it," Athan replied. "This place is weird."

"Now you admit it?" Deva asked.

"Never denied it. I just don't believe it's what you think."

"Enough," Kale said. "We can debate this place after we have more facts. Arguing opinions is pointless. Thaina, get those fighters launched. Wena, open a com net for the various parties that need to talk. Meira's preparing a team so we should as well. I want ten soldiers to accompany whoever goes down there."

Deva raised her hand. "I volunteer."

Athan chuckled. "Your eagerness is ridiculous. Don't you want to know more before you risk your life?"

"That's how we're going to learn more," Deva replied.

"I'll be selecting the people who go," Kale said. "Focus on your duties, both of you. We've got too much going on for this kind of banter."

"Sorry, sir," Athan began moving the ship and Deva tapped away in silence. Kale knew he had to pick those who *wanted* to go on the mission. There would be plenty of people who weren't interested. The soldiers tended to be good sports about any sort of trip but any others, technicians or people like Deva, were less enthusiastic.

As the fighters launched, Kale hoped they found what they needed with minimal effort. Flying around down there might even be strange depending on the atmosphere. They'd learn a great deal from a few passes. Luckily, that's all they needed to decide how to progress to the next step.

"Deva, have you been able to analyze the buoy?"

"I've been working on it. As I said, it seems to be functioning…seems to be. I still say we get someone out there to work on it."

"Understood." Kale hit the com and brought Meira online. "I need you to get a technician who can fix a com buoy. The one in this system is acting up."

"They'll be ready to go shortly. I'll have them report to the hangar."

"Perfect." Kale turned it off. "Thaina, prepare a second shuttle for the repair of that buoy. We need to be hitting our problems from multiple angles if we're going to get out of here. Okay, I'll be quiet and let you work now. Let me know the moment you have something to report."

***

Vinthari Alma Il'Var had been flying a fighter stationed on The Crystal Font since long before Anthar Ru'Xin assumed command. She started her career as a Zanthari and took a promotion just before their ill-fated trip to the research outpost. The whole mission left her with a bad feeling and the gravity of their jump out of the system confirmed her fears.

Arriving in the unknown sector with a broken down buoy and a strange planet didn't do much to improve her confidence. Her duty, along with two other fighters, was to perform recon and gather additional scan data before a team landed on the surface. She didn't envy them, especially since she had no particular desire to see what happened when they broke atmosphere.

They departed the ship in a group of six with a shuttle craft in tow. All of them escorted the larger vessel to the buoy, flying at a somewhat leisurely pace. The shuttle didn't have the thrust of the fighters and even if it did, the technician aboard likely had no desire to have a thrill ride. Alma struggled with boredom, watching her scanner, half wishing they were on a combat mission.

Her wingmen included Zanthari Rahan Ti'Vane and Zanthari Hilot Va'Doth. They'd flown with her since they joined the ship two missions prior and proved to be quite good, especially during the action over the research facility. The Crystal Font was their first assignment but they shed their green status quickly.

The shuttle slowed and attached itself to the buoy and it's primary escorts took up positions around it. Alma and her two companions departed, heading for the planet at a quick pace. She patched in to the bridge, communicating directly with the chief tech officer who could guide them if necessary.

"We're approaching the surface now," Alma announced. "Can you give me a safe vector? I need a window."

"Actually," Deva's voice crackled in her speaker, "you don't. Double check your scanners before committing but from here, it looks like you can just fly right down there."

"That seems impossible," Alma replied. "Are you sure about your figures?"

"As sure as I can be considering the place and how strange it is. Do what you can, please. Keep your scanners on full so I can acquire the data."

Alma felt extremely skeptical but didn't argue. She increased speed, closing the distance to break atmosphere. As they approached, she expected heat to react to the shields but nothing happened, not for some time. The scans didn't make sense. They hadn't even hit an oxygen patch yet and when it happened a few moments later, the reaction was mild to say the least.

The shields barely flared up.

This is bizarre. The briefing said strange but that's an understatement.

The sky turned blue and she broke through light cloud coverage, revealing a vast landscape of glistening hills, forests and a sea off to the east. Rahan gasped into the com. "This place is spectacular…" He spoke in awe. "I didn't expect it."

"Not from the briefing," Hilot said, sounding far less impressed. "I expected it to be a little more...mechanized I guess."

"We're looking for a structure," Alma said. "Something that houses the power we need. My scanners aren't picking up anything like that so I guess we're doing some flying. Spread out for maximum coverage. Deva's going to want as much data as we can get."

She took up the center with the others falling out until they were barely within visual range. Alma relaxed into her seat, allowing the computer to collect all the data they needed. She directed her attention to the water. It stretched off to the horizon, not broken up by islands or any other obstruction.

It reminded her of an ocean near where she grew up. Her father taught her to sail there and the memory made her a little sad. She hadn't visited home in a while, even before the jump incident. Pretty much everyone on board prepared to die when they drew the enemy away from the Earth ship. Despite the tactical necessity, the Anthar didn't realize how sour some of the crew had become over the decision.

Making such a call is his job but it didn't have to be popular.

Her scanner pinged, drawing her attention back to the monitor. Four dots appeared, moving quickly toward them. "Are you two picking those up?"

"Affirmative, ma'am," Rahan said. "I'm trying to get some details now."

"They're...no!" Hilot cursed. "Those are enemy fighters!"

"*The* enemy?" Alma couldn't believe it. "That's not possible! The Font would've picked up a battleship out there. This literally can't be possible!"

"I'm afraid it is," Rahan replied.

"Deva," Alma asked, "are you picking up any enemy capital ships overhead?"

"Negative," Deva replied. "What are you seeing?"

Alma sent the data up to her. They would close to firing range shortly. "Combat shields up. I think we're about to be engaged."

"Are they on a course for you?" Deva asked.

"Yes," Rahan answered. "They're flying right for us!"

"We're on this," Alma said. "If more come though, we're going to need reinforcements."

"I'm on it," Deva said. "Just be careful."

Hardly an appropriate wish considering what we're about to do. Alma saw the vapor trails of the fighters ahead, grayish-white streams signaling their approach. They still weren't close enough to see but they'd be there soon. They flew in an attack formation, picking up speed. They couldn't maneuver as wildly in the atmosphere as space but they'd definitely push some Gs to get an advantageous position.

"Follow my lead," Alma said. "I'm going to dive, get closer to the surface and draw them after me. You take up the rear and get a firing solution. We need to at least even the odds as quickly as possible. Do not hold back."

"Understood." The other pilots answered together, both climbing as Alma plunged her flight stick forward.

The force pressed her into her seat as she rocketed toward the ground. Shortly, the sky left her vision and her altimeter began warning her about collision. At less than two hundred feet, she pulled up, leveling out to fly toward the mountains to the west. Her companions would fly around up above, waiting for the enemy to make their move.

And they didn't have to wait long.

All four fighters went after her, closing in and firing the moment they were in range. Alma's shields doubled up in the back and she performed evasive maneuvers, dodging left and right to avoid their blasts. She remained calm, forcing herself into a state of severe focus. Blasts struck the rocks ahead of her and she banked left, skimming along the side of the mountain and keeping it to her right.

The enemy flew after her, one of them bouncing off the rocks. Its shields flared as it tried to recover, spinning out of control for a moment before leveling off and rejoining the fight. He was rewarded with two missiles from one of Alma's companions, both striking him from the top. The ship exploded, bits of debris scattering throughout the forest.

The other three didn't give up, continuing after Alma with all the determination of a hungry child. She continued her maneuvers, finally taking a pair of shots that knocked her shields down to sixty percent. Diving again, she went below one hundred feet then had to climb to avoid a set of particularly tall trees.

One of the enemies trimmed the tops of the tallest branches and broke formation, flying off to the South. "He's trying to get behind us," Rahan said.

"I'll take him," Alma replied, banking hard to find a firing solution. The other two didn't give up on her, staying on her tale but as she came around on their companion, they tried to close the distance. Fortunately, alliance fighters seemed a *little* faster than theirs and she kept them away.

Her computer gave her tone and she fired missiles and guns, laying into the enemy just as he fired some blasts. He never could've hit Rahan or Hilot, they were barely even in front of him but his random shots struck the rocks and scattered bits into the valley. Alma's attack, on the other hand, obliterated him, causing his core to explode.

The other two broke and started to run, flying back the way they came. "After them!" Alma shouted. "But don't shoot. Let's see where they're going."

"What could they even be doing down here?" Rahan asked. "This doesn't make any sense!"

"I know." Alma shook her head. "But we have to figure it out. If there's an enemy presence here, this operation just took a dramatic turn. Stay on them. They can't go far."

***

"Anthar," Deva turned in her seat to address Kale, "our fighters have engaged *enemy* ships on the surface!"

"What?" Kale stood up. "Are you sure?"

Deva put footage on the main screen for him to see and they all watched as the fighters began a massive fight. While that went on, she checked her console to see whether or not the shuttle was in any trouble but so far, it seemed fine. The technician was working on the buoy, unaware of the violence going on below them.

"Do you have any enemy capital ships on the scanners?" Kale asked.

"No, sir. Nothing. We're the only ship in this system."

"They must've crashed down there," Athan said. "And now they're trying to defend themselves."

"If they crashed, they'd be insane to attack us," Kale replied. "Once we find their main camp, they'd be helpless to bombardment. Why would they even reveal themselves?"

"Maybe they knew we'd find them one way or another," Deva said.

"I can get a firing solution when we find them," Thaina added. "Give me some coordinates and we'll go to town."

"Hold on," Kale said. "If they're holding the power source we need, we can't destroy the entire area. We have to take a step back from this. Consider what's going on and what we need. This is bigger than a fight. How're our pilots doing?"

"They've taken two down..." Deva paused. "Sir, they're pursuing the others. Vinthari Il'Var has had her pilots stand down so they can determine where the enemy came from."

"Good." Kale nodded. "I'm glad she's thinking that way. Stay in contact with her and put the shuttle's escorts on alert. Alma might need some help if they encounter a larger force. In fact, have the rest of our fighters get out there just in case. I'd rather be overkill in this situation. Considering how far out in the middle of nowhere we appear to be, prudence doesn't seem wise."

***

Alma and the others chased after the enemies so far that they ended up in the middle of the night on the planet. Her scanners picked up a strange formation of rock ahead, towering up higher than the mountain itself. Image enhancement showed it to be smooth, as if carved out of stone with openings all across the surface.

We found what we're looking for and our enemy is already here. Fantastic.

She fed it back to the ship and collected as much data as possible. The energy readings were off the chart. Whatever created the constant pulse of power came from inside that place. Flying over, she noted that there were no enemy ships down there. No shuttles. No wreckage. The two fighters they chased seemed to wink off radar as well.

They must be using the energy signature to mask themselves.

"Deva, we might have a problem. As you can see, we've got a structure but it must be blocking our scans. I can't even see the people we were chasing now."

"Understood. Please return to orbit and await further orders."

"Are you sure that's a good idea?" Alma asked. "It seems like we should be patrolling the area just in case."

"We're working out a strategy right now," Deva replied. "Thank you for the suggestion. Get back to orbit."

Yes, ma'am. The thought carried sarcasm but her response remained professional. "On our way." She directed her two wings to follow her and they left the area, climbing away from the surface.

Alma thought the situation felt odd when they arrived but looking at it now, she felt considerable alarm about it all. If the enemy got hold of the type of energy that planet seemed to be producing, if they could somehow apply it to the war effort, then the alliance would very much be in trouble.

Considering Anthar Ru'Xin's penchant for doing *whatever it took* to keep the enemy from key objectives, Alma began to worry about what might happen to them all if they were truly stranded out there. She hoped he didn't decide to detonate the ship and the planet with it to prevent them their prize.

Chapter 5

Gray felt serious reservations about moving so close to the system they left a large enemy presence behind in but he agreed with the tech crew's assessment. They needed to gather data and what better place to do so than from the place they left? Returning to the scene of the crime would've been the best route but impractical.

As they winked into the quiet system, Olly immediately performed a system scan using the buoy in place to check for any ships that might've recently jumped in. They were alone with only a few uninhabitable planets nearby for company. The tech team dug in to gather their data and Gray did his best not to focus on the bad feeling rising in the back of his mind.

He didn't fully understand how the alliance buoys worked but based on what his people were trying to do, it made sense that the enemy might be able to use them in a similar way. If that were the case, they might be monitoring those around that centralized, secret research facility and if so, they'd know that someone just hopped in nearby.

It wouldn't take them long to investigate so the situation became burdened with urgency.

Adam had Revente ready the pilots and they were on standby in the event of needing to launch for an attack. Search and rescue crafts were prepped as well for when they found The Crystal Font. They might be dead in space, unable to travel at all and in that case, Gray had to be prepared to save lives.

The medical centers were also fully stocked and on alert standby. Gray prepared for the worst and prayed for the best but considering how long they'd been alone, he could not quite muster much in the way of positivity. When the Behemoth suffered a jump failure due to sabotage, they were back in less than three days.

Months seemed impossible to recover from. If not due to damage or attack, supplies could've run out. They might've starved to death long before any other peril took their lives. The thought that they escaped destruction only to die through some lingering means filled Gray with rage. The unfairness of it stuck in his craw.

"Captain, I've finished the assessment," Olly announced. "The adjacent system has been abandoned. There are no enemy ships to speak of in left. They must've looted everything they could and departed."

"What about the anomaly we were looking for?" Clea asked. "Did you find anything to do with that?"

"Paul's feeding us data back now."

Gray watched Clea focus on her tablet for a long moment, nodding several times.

"They did dump their pulse drive waste," Clea announced. "There's so much radiation in that area, it might even be impacting the planet surface. We'd need to send a clean up ship to make that area safe. Shields might not even help for long."

"Wow..." Gray shook his head. "I'll keep that tactic in mind...and the repercussions."

"So we know they did it," Olly said. "But what's that mean for us getting their location?"

"Unfortunately, with these readings?" Clea sighed. "They could practically be anywhere. It might've thrown them off course to another galaxy as far as we know. Our only hope now is to find something in the buoy. I guarantee the system here doesn't get much traffic. I'm downloading the logs now."

"Will that lead us to them?" Gray asked.

"I'm assuming it will lead us to the next buoy, sir," Clea replied. "We have to follow the bread crumbs as they say."

"Ah, you learned our fairy tale."

Clea shrugged. "Seemed a good place to start."

"Captain," Olly interrupted, his voice urgent. "I've got someone jumping into this sector! Buoy just activated."

"On screen."

They watched as a ship winked in, a medium sized cargo vessel that had seen better days. Gray checked his computer to see what ID it was using but the information came back garbled. *Pirate*.

"That ship's armed," Olly said. "No identification. They're hailing us."

"Oh, this will be rich," Gray said. "Put them on. Maybe they've seen The Crystal Font."

"This is Rigis Tor'Eray," a male's voice piped through their speakers. "We don't have a quarrel with you. We'd like to just go on our way."

"We're not looking for you," Gray said. "But considering what you're doing, we can't just let you leave to torment some unarmed ship elsewhere in the galaxy."

"Look, we're not pirates," Rigis replied. "We're just doing some salvage runs on the down low. Trying to make a little extra money. You know how it is. It's hard making a living out here without you guys giving us a hard time."

"Have you salvaged an alliance ship?" Gray asked. "Specifically, a battle cruiser?"

Rigis laughed. "If we did, do you think I'd tell you? Or that we'd be flying around in this hunk of garbage? That would've been a big prize. No, we were checking out rumors of some research facility in the nearby system but it was totally ransacked and destroyed. Nothing there to take."

Gray cut the signal for a moment and turned to Olly. "Check their story. Check the database for any reports that might match this ship for piracy. If they're just scavengers, I think we can give them a pass but I don't trust this guy."

"On it, sir."

"How would they hear rumors about that secret location?" Gray asked.

Clea shrugged. "Anyone could've leaked info about it after our trip. The soldiers, some of the researchers...if they even told a loved one it could've turned into a hint."

"So much for secrets." Gray turned the com back on. "You didn't find any hostiles in that sector, huh? How long were you there for?"

"Two days. Nearly ran out of supplies so we're heading back to a friendly port. That's a legal place."

"Not with that ID you're not," Gray said. "You know as well as I do they won't let you dock anywhere without a legal registration."

"We…" Rigis coughed. "We have one."

"Uh huh. Don't try to leave. We're confirming a few things." Gray turned off the com and looked at Adam. "Battle stations but keep it subtle. I don't want these guys trying to run before we can secure some information."

Adam nodded and turned to his own com. Olly glanced back. "Sir, I do have reports of a ship that matches this description attacking the shipping lanes. Last week, they took down an ore shipment being sent to a colony that needed it pretty bad. They killed the entire crew, stole the goods, stripped the vessel and let the hull drift."

"Bastards." Gray scowled then contacted them again. "Listen, Rigis. We know you've been out pirating. This is how we're going to play this. Surrender to us and you'll be arrested. No one gets hurt. If you choose not to, we will open fire and judging by the size of your ship…well, let's just say I'm pretty sure you won't get a day in court."

"We've got more bite than bark," Rigis replied. "You don't want to do this."

"So I'm guessing that means you don't want to surrender?" Gray asked. "Are you sure about that?"

"We're ready to repel you," Rigis said. "Good luck."

The com went dead.

"They're powering up their weapons," Olly said. "Scanning…they seem pretty standard. No credible threat."

"Reddings," Gray said, "light them up."

"Yes, sir." Reddings opened fire, letting loose a barrage from the cannons. The pirate retaliated at the same time, laying into them with their own blasts. The impact caused the Behemoth's shields to flare but no appreciable damage. They didn't so much as tremble from the blow.

In contrast, when the Behemoth's pulse blasts struck the pirate's port side, their shields flared and winked out. Six blasts struck the hull directly, carving neat and perfect holes into the metal. Flames bloomed out, perfect globes of orange quickly dissipating as some emergency measure sealed the breach.

"They want to talk," Agatha announced. "They're hailing us."

"I bet they do." Gray nodded to her. "Put them on."

Rigis spoke the moment the com connected, "okay, so…hold on. Just…hold on. I think we can come to some agreement. Let's just…slow down."

"Are you prepared to surrender?" Gray asked.

Olly lifted his hand. "Sir, they're priming their jump drive! They're looking at less than twenty seconds to departure!"

"Redding, target the drive and fire."

"Um…they've shot something," Clea said. "Olly, check those. I'm reading unstable mass."

"Pulse bombs!" Olly shouted. "They've fired them from their ship!"

"Sneaky bastards, belay the last order," Gray said. "Target those bombs and take them out. Now!"

"AI turrets are already engaging," Redding said. "Three down…make that four. Five…six!"

"What did they do, unload their entire payload?" Adam turned to his monitor. "That's it. They're done."

Gray watched his own monitor as the shockwave from the bombs slammed into the pirate's vessel. They listed, careening to starboard and began to drift. Their coms dropped instantly and the lights on the surface went out. If anyone survived the attack, they likely had less than a few minutes left to live.

"Olly?" Gray asked. "What've you got?"

"Major hull breach. Minimal life support. Engines are totally offline." Olly shook his head. "They're on generators, sir. I'm estimating they'll be out of power in less than twenty minutes."

"Life signs?"

"Also minimal." Olly paused. "I'm reading ten people." He glanced over his shoulder. "There were forty when we did our initial scan."

Gray nodded. "Understood. Agatha, get a message to them. We'll take them aboard. Adam, launch search and rescue to bring them aboard."

"There's a chance their core might melt down," Clea said. "If so, it's going to blow. That could put our shuttle in jeopardy."

"I get it. We'll make it fast." Gray turned. "Did they reply to us?"

"They're ready to comply," Agatha said. "They're making their way out of the ship in their escape pods."

"Excellent. Collect them." Gray gestured to Clea. "Make sure the tech team takes advantage of this down time with those buoys. We'll be here for a short time. Figure out as much as you can before we're ready to go. Maybe we'll get lucky with the Crystal Font. Get to work, folks. We're going to have a busy shift."

***

Paul joined Olly on the bridge, carrying his tablet with him. They spoke quietly, performing a variety of checks on the buoy. Outside, search and rescue moved to assist the pirates, their efforts full of far more stress than the two tech officers experienced. Olly tried to ignore it but despite the fact that the men were criminals, he couldn't handle the thought of them suffocating.

They could've died in a massive core explosion. At least those ten lived...though they might be pretty bad off.

"I think I found the message," Paul said. He played it at a low volume. *This is the Crystal Font requesting immediate assistance. We've experienced a jump malfunction and are currently located—*. The message was cut short just before they could offer the coordinates. They exchanged a look.

"Okay, good. So we know it came this way." Olly checked the cache and unlike the one in the high traffic area, this one barely had any messages at all. Certainly not enough to purge them any time soon. He hoped they were tough to crack. They had access codes but if anyone had the ability to hop in and track people, these things represented a serious security breach.

He brought up the list of buoys in the area, all connecting to this one. The research facility came up first on the list but luckily, it was off and could not have been used. Another one in an even less inhabited system linked up to this one going even further out from the core of alliance civilization.

Such places might be brought into the fold of colonization in the future but at least for the time being they were impractical to protect. In recent years, the only places the alliance bothered to settle were close enough to get a military presence there quickly. While jump tech allowed a ship to arrive in time to help, messages were not instantaneous.

Of course, that didn't matter to the colonies the Orion's Light took out.

Olly got the coordinates for the next buoy and sent them over to Ensign Leonard Marcus, their navigator. He'd have to come up with a decent jump point entry so they could check the next buoy. How many would they have to try before they tracked down the Crystal Font? Olly worried they would eventually come to a high enough traffic device that the trail would go cold.

This trail of bread crumbs had its own threat of birds to eat.

"You okay?" Paul asked.

Olly nodded. "Just thinking ahead…or trying to at least."

"I understand." Paul scratched his head. "This seems pretty intense but at least we have another place to check out."

"So far so good." Olly glanced back at Clea and considered giving her a quick briefing. She was busy coordinating the retrieval of the pirates with Commander Everly. Their new prisoners probably all needed medical attention before spending the rest of their time in the brig. He decided to leave her be and sent the report to her mailbox. "We've done our part."

"I'm heading back to the tech lab," Paul said. "I'll try to come up with another way to track these messages. I'm not confident but hey, we've found stranger things, right?"

"Every time we leave space dock." Olly grinned but the expression was forced. "See you later, man."

"Olly," Gray called out as Paul left the bridge. "I trust with Mister Baily's departure, you have a new destination for us."

"Yes, sir. I sent it to Leonard."

"Very good." Gray clapped his hands. "Where are we with grabbing those pirates?"

"Nearly done, sir," Adam said. "The last escape pod has been collected and they're bringing them on board now. I'd say we've got another fifteen minutes."

"Any chance to shorten that?"

Adam shook his head. "Not safely. The shuttle's towing all those in. It's simply going to take that much time to get back to the ship and land."

"Okay. Leonard, I want a course by the time they're on board. As soon as they report in, Redding will initiate the jump. Agatha, give the crew a head's up that we're getting out of here and report in the derelict ship drifting out here. I'd rather our people scavenge that thing than risk another pirate crew coming in here for an easy mark."

Olly went to work, his stomach doing flips. The time pressure weighed on him heavily. Every minute and hour that ticked by, the Crystal Font might be lost. Worse, in the back of him mind, he knew they might already be gone. It had been far too long for a starship to survive out there without support.

Much as he didn't want to admit it, he felt like they were chasing a ghost ship.

Olly never bothered to pray before but as they prepped to jump out of the system, he took a moment to put out some positive energy. He affirmed his hope that they'd find their companions alive, perhaps battered but otherwise well off. Even without precedent or facts, he tried to will it to be true.

This feels a lot better than being pessimistic. Come on, guys. Don't let us down. You showed so much spirit when we were fighting over the research facility. That kind of will can't simply be killed by something so paltry as being lost in space for a while. We'll find you. One way or another. Just hang in there.

***

Kale stared at the imagery taken by Alma's ship. The structure they discovered climbed into the sky some sixty stories. The land around it appeared to be cleared away, flattened and void of trees. None of the snapshots the pilots took, none of their video revealed enemy presence but they *knew* they were down there...somewhere.

He sent a patrol around the planet to ensure they didn't miss something, checking for a hidden vessel. *Maybe they came up with a way to trick sensors since we've been gone. There aren't many explanations.* But the enemy fighters didn't go back to orbit, they disappeared around the structure.

They might've been destroyed but there was no evidence to support the thought. According to scans and surveillance, the four enemies didn't even exist. Deva couldn't even find the debris of the two downed vessels but they saw the video footage of the fight and knew it happened.

Without the in flight cameras, Kale might've questioned Alma and her team's sanity. Hell, she was already second guessing what happened. Whatever happened didn't make a lot of sense but they knew three important facts. One, they *had* to get down there to get the power necessary to leave. Two, enemy presence complicated the mission. Three, they were dealing with a relatively small bit of opposition.

After all, how many of them could be down there without their ship giving off *some* sign? A capital ship couldn't have landed on the planet anyway and if it crashed, the place wouldn't be nearly as well off. Kale decided they would make their move but it would be with a large force of soldiers, ready for whatever action they might encounter.

He stood and joined Wena at the com station, tapping into the whole ship. "This is the Anthar speaking. I'm sure some of you have heard we encountered an enemy presence on this planet. We have performed extensive scouting in and around the area but have not located a capital ship. Whoever is down there, they are alone and cannot be numerous.

"We *must* take the area and get what we've come for. This is our way home. I intend to get you there. It will require a team to go to the surface and I'm putting together those people now. Please continue to focus on your duties and I promise you, we'll get out of here as soon as possible. Direct any questions to section leads and they can contact me directly. Thank you."

Kale killed the com and turned to Deva. "This is against my better judgement," he said, "but I need you to go on this mission."

"What?" Deva's eyes went wide. "Are you serious? You're letting me go?"

"You've got the best chance of figuring anything out down there...the best chance to get us that power source. But there might be fighting, Deva."

Deva nodded. "Understood." Her enthusiasm dipped. "I...I've never been in a combat situation before. Not on the ground."

"I know. You'll have plenty of support. And if things are too crazy..." Kale shrugged. "We'll bring you back and find another way out of here."

"There is no other way," Athan said. "Right?"

"Not that we've explored," Kale replied. "How's the buoy work going?"

Deva snapped her fingers. "Let me check in with them...wait. They've sent a report. Sending to your station now."

Kale read the information, frowning. He half expected the news. The buoy should've been operating normally. Nothing about it indicated damage or malfunction. The power source was good and it definitely took their message. However, it did not say whether it transmitted it nor had it received any messages for some time.

Perfect. It might've worked, it might not have. Much like those enemy fighters. They were there, we have proof but now they're not. We can't be cautious, not now. It's time to act.

"Go ahead and get ready, Deva. I'll have Varez take your place."

Deva offered a quick salute and hurried off the bridge.

"You made her career," Thaina quipped.

"She joined the military thinking we were in another era," Kale said. "She's an explorer first, a soldier...maybe third. But don't worry, she'll get the job done."

"I'm not worried," Thaina said. "Terrified about being stuck? Yes, but worry? I can't remember when last we had the luxury of something so low key."

Kale smiled and shook his head. "Well put, Thaina. I'm going to see the team off. Athan, you have the bridge."

***

Search and rescue spent two hours retrieving the various pirate escape pods. When they brought them on board, all but two required serious medical attention. They were secured in one of the medical wings under guard until they could be safely transported to the brig, where they'd wait to be transferred to alliance authorities.

Gray got them out of there the moment everyone was stowed away, jumping to the next buoy on the list. Tech crews once again stripped everything they could from the sector and followed the bread crumbs to the next location, which continued to lead them further away from any civilized space.

After five jumps, they needed to slow down and take a shift for the crew to recover. Even with the enhanced drive and improvements made by the alliance and later Durant, there was still a cost to so much FTL travel. The downtime gave them all a chance to evaluate what they'd learned so far, while attempting to make an educated guess about their destination.

Adam took the bridge so Gray could get some rest but he had a hard time falling asleep as he considered their mission. Seven total jumps meant an entire day's worth of shifts so far. He didn't expect to locate the Crystal Font quickly, but that didn't quell his sense of urgency. Every hour they spent looking was another that might end with them locating a ghost ship.

It seems strangely convenient that the message ends the way it does.

Having the coordinates cut off felt suspicious but Gray didn't know what the purpose would be. Other than to waste someone's time looking, the government may not have even sent anyone. The fact that they were out there on a scavenger hunt couldn't have been anticipated. And if an enemy wanted to ambush someone, they needed to tell the potential rescuers where to go.

Gray fell into a fitful sleep and woke feeling worse than when he started. After a quick refresh, change of clothes and a meal, his overall mood improved but he had to fight hard against a sense of helplessness. He could not show his crew that he didn't believe in the mission. They had to be devoted to the search or it would be a futile effort.

When he arrived on the bridge, Adam relinquished command and gave him a quick update. "Clea and the others have found our next destination," he said. "Leonard's put in the coordinates and we're ready to go on your mark."

Gray sat down and took in a deep breath, putting on his best 'confident' expression. "You heard them, Redding. Let's get out of here."

***

Deva sat on the shuttle trying not to tap her foot, feeling a mixture of excitement and anxiety in equal measures. She'd visited alien worlds before but they were always colonized or somehow tamed. This one, a place so shrouded in mystery, might've been the single greatest find of her generation. And she would be one of the first kielans to set foot on the surface.

The others around her, six soldiers, were well armed with assault rifles, pistols and grenades. They were prepared for serious war with the enemy and their silence made her feel like a fool. Each person around her exuded more quiet determination than any thrill. The threat of combat did strange things to people.

She turned to look out the window just as they broke atmosphere. She marveled at the minimal impact the shields took from the venture and as they leveled out into the clear sky, her curiosity only increased. Checking the scans, the readings once again defied any science she understood.

As Athan said, without some resistance, the planet should be a wasteland, pock marked with meteorite strikes. Instead, the surface looked like a preservation park back home. Beside naturally occurring damage from space debris, Deva still didn't have any sign of a crashed ship. The enemy could not have landed there so how did they cover up what had to be a tragedy?

Trees covered the horizon, rising up the hills and into the valleys. Imagery from the pilot's recon showed that the ground around their destination was cleared out, flattened and mostly dirt. There must've been something beneath it, perhaps even concrete or ground down stone but they wouldn't have proof until they landed.

The structure came into view and Deva gasped, using the camera on her helmet to grab footage as they flew in. She wished she sat in the front to get a better view. The height of the thing, the grandeur almost made her cry. Kielans built things just as impressive in a way but this held a majesty to it, a glory enhanced by the secrets hidden within.

Vinthari Lhar Xi'Reth commanded the soldiers. He was technically Deva's peer but on the ground, he would have operational control. She gladly accepted his leadership in this regard, especially if weapons started firing. They gave her a rifle but she hadn't fired one since her last fitness test over a year ago.

"Taking us in near those rocks," Lhar said. "Have our escorts continue to check the area. I have a bad feeling about this landing. It could be an ambush. Everyone, Vinthari Thi'Noch is our VIP. She's the only person who can get what we need out of this trip so I want her protected *the whole time*. Vali and Niersa, she's your responsibility."

Deva never met the two. Vali was a big guy, someone who clearly worked out. In his suit, he looked like a giant. Niersa, in perfect contrast, was a wiry woman who looked capable of snapping a person in half. They didn't reply verbally, just nodded and exchanged looks. Deva was grateful she couldn't see their expressions through their helmets.

Something told her that escort duty annoyed these people.

"The rest of you will be on fire first duty," Lhar continued. "If you see the enemy, there's no hesitation. Whatever they're doing down here, we'll figure out after they're dead. Take aim, fire and make your shots count. We've got work to do down here and if it's not completed, we don't go home. You get me?"

The five soldiers shouted an affirmation at the same time, making Deva wince as the speakers in her helmet crackled. *If this is what it's going to be like to be in a fight, I'm not prepared.*

A little fear tickled her anxiety and excitement.

The shuttle descended suddenly and Deva grabbed the handle over her head, wondering if they'd been hit. Were they about to crash? Had something happened? Why didn't she feel an impact? A thousand possibilities entered her mind before she thought to use her scanner but by then it was too late.

The ship lurched again, this time slowing down. The back ramp dropped and their safety harnesses disengaged. Lhar began shouting, "go, go, go!" Each of the soldiers leapt into action, rushing out of the ship and out onto the surface. Deva hesitated, watching them go as they lifted their weapons and started securing the area.

"This isn't break time, Thi'Noch!" Lhar yelled at her. "Go!"

Deva stumbled to her feet and rushed out, having to hop at the very end of the ramp, which hovered over the ground a few feet. She nearly fell but strong hands grabbed her by the arm and dragged her to the nearby rocks, depositing her in some cover. The shuttle took off and fighters circled overhead.

We're really doing this! Deva tried to control her breathing, desperate not to hyperventilate. Adrenaline threatened to overwhelm her. She could barely see, wondering if someone with a gun might be aiming in her direction at that very moment. *Do I need to scan or get out of my weapon?*

"Contact!" Niersa yelled. "Northwest! Motion."

Oh Fates, this is happening! They're really here! But how did we not see them? How? I don't get it! This planet must be masking their presence. Deva forced herself to look at the scanner, tuning it to the new position on the surface. *I have to figure out what's going on…and focus.* The soldiers continued shouting around her, moving into position. *This is going to be tough.*

***

Lhar didn't look forward to the assignment. He'd run many missions involving alien worlds, fighting in places he never set foot on, but he was never a pioneer. When they landed on that planet, his briefing warned him they might encounter the enemy but it didn't make sense. How did they get there?

Regardless, he went ready for a fight. However, contact within seconds of the shuttle lifting off? That shocked him. They took cover as pulse blasts shattered rocks around them, cutting into the walls. Lhar gave quick hand gesture orders, directing his people into different positions while keeping their heads down.

He checked his scanner without revealing himself, remaining in cover to see what they were up against. It took the device a moment to catch up then showed him seven foot soldiers in a scattered formation, something that struck him as odd. They never stood in one place. They ran around, quick and swift in their motions.

This time, they stood their ground, popping shots at them.

"Trias," Lhar shouted, "put down some cover fire! Bleise, use it to flank. Once you're in position, the rest of us will hit them! Go!"

Trias popped up and opened up, pealing off several bursts. Bleise counted to five aloud then dashed away from them, moving to the next rock formation over. Pulse blasts caught the ground around him, nearly taking him out. He dove, hit the ground and rolled into cover, pressing his back against the stone.

"You call that cover?" He shouted back.

"They don't care that I'm shooting at them!" Trias replied with a grunt. "Not sure what you want me to do if they're ignoring me!"

Lhar looked just in time to see her catch one of the enemies in the face, knocking him to the ground. Blood pooled around him and his death made his companions break off, finally moving for cover. This gave Bleise his chance to get to his position and Lhar took the opportunity to direct the other soldiers to advance.

They broke free, all but Niersa and Vali who remained with Deva. Each of them led with their weapons firing in an attempt to keep their opponent's heads down. As they rushed forward, pulse blasts cut into the ground around them. Yuris took a shot to the side and was tossed through the air, landing hard behind them. He remained still, not even wallowing in pain.

Lhar fired a shot at the top of one of the enemy's heads, the only part peeking out from behind stone cover. One of his three blasts connected, searing off the armor and melting through the top of his skull. Flopping backwards, his weapon went flying and skid on the ground, sliding toward a flight of stairs.

Each of the kielans made it to another set of rocks for cover just as Bleise opened up on the enemy's flank. Screams filled the air as he took down at least a couple of them. Lhar called into his com to back off, to take cover again but Bleise seemed determined to finish them off on his own. Lhar stood and fired as well, ordering the others to cover him.

It didn't work. One of the aliens caught Bleise in the chest just below his neck, dropping him to the ground. A strangled cry rang out and he went still, quite dead. "No!" Lhar shot the one who killed his soldier, finishing him off before aiming at the next. He noted the bodies on the ground and counted them.

Eleven. What? There were only six!

"Deva! What's going on? Where are they coming from?"

"I don't know!" Deva shouted back. "They just...appear on the scans!"

"New tech?" Vali offered. "It must be. Some kind of ability to bend light and keep themselves invisible, right?"

"No way," Deva said. "Not in the short time we've been gone. We would've seen prototypes. They would've used during the fight at the research facility. This is something else. I guarantee it!"

Lhar checked his scanner and noted there were still four enemies out there. *Fifteen? That's more like what I would've expected...*

Another one went down and the other three made a break for it, running for the stairs.

Wait, they're running? Lhar felt incredibly confused. "Shoot!"

His men fired, taking down the rest of them as they went. Each body collapsed on the stairs, sliding down to the base. Lhar approached the nearest corpse and nudged it with his foot. *It's real enough*. He motioned for the others to approach. "Deva, get over here and scan this. What am I looking at?"

The tech officer hurried over, crouching the entire way. When she arrived, she dropped down to a knee and looked all around, especially checking the rocks above them. Lhar rolled his eyes but he knew she had good cause to be nervous. There *could* be more out there somewhere. The fact they hadn't attacked while their friends died though made it unlikely.

"Um...this armor is strange." Deva sighed. "I don't know *what* this is! It doesn't appear to be one of the enemies we've ever fought before."

"What are you talking about?" Lhar asked. "That's impossible. It must be."

"It's...wait!" Deva stood up suddenly as the body seemed to dissolve into thin air. "It's gone! Oh my...it's...it's pure energy! This thing was a construct of energy!"

"That doesn't even make sense," Niersa said. "How could that be possible?"

Deva shrugged. "I have no idea! I...I should check the others."

Lhar stopped her. "Vali can handle the medical stuff. You focus on what we need. We didn't come down here and potentially lose two people for you to waste time. Find the energy and figure out a way for us to tap it so we can get out of here as soon as possible. Understood?"

Deva nodded. "Yes, sir. I'm on it."

"Good." Lhar turned to the others. "Form a perimeter. I'm going to report back to the ship on what we just discovered. Fates know they're going to love this. It's definitely not what anyone expected...and now we know there's no way to anticipate what we might encounter next. Stay on your guard. It might get uglier."

***

Chapter 6

Clea sat in her room working on a computer, trying to piece together where they should go next. The same garbled message greeted them at every location they visited, proving the caches of these buoys rarely got purged. After half an hour, she felt no more confident about saving their friends than she had when they started.

A knock on her door made her sigh. She didn't feel like distractions at the moment but called out for the person to come in. Durant entered and immediately sat down, looking smug. Her mood must've showed because his expression melted and he sat up straight, clearing his throat before speaking.

"I've analyzed the schematics for that weapon those terrorists used on us. It's pretty ingenious. I have to give props to Novalat."

"I'm sure they'll be thrilled," Clea replied. "Have you countered it then?"

"Well, it's harder to do that than you think," Durant said. "The shields already have to be down for it to work. That means we need to do something with our armor if we want to reflect it. I've got the computer going through the different options on how that might work but I have to be honest, retrofitting armor is a lot harder than reprogramming shields."

"Meaning it won't be as easy to prepare for this one."

"Correct." Durant leaned forward. "What're you working on?"

"Trying to figure out where the Crystal Font is still." Clea shrugged. "I've been at it for hours too but we're just plunging deeper into space. I want some more certainty, Durant. I want to know where they could've possibly gone. Already, we're seventeen systems away from the research facility. I really doubt they *planned* this far of a jump."

"They probably jumped again as soon as they appeared."

"Not if they jumped so close to their trap," Clea pointed out.

"Perhaps...but we can't know how much damage they experienced. It might've been minimal. And it has been a *long* time...relatively speaking."

"Yes, but..." Clea looked at her screen and paused. She'd been searching for buoys that might have the message but considering they didn't get the entire communication, an idea hit her. "What if they are somewhere with a malfunctioning buoy?"

"Because we don't have the complete message?"

Clea nodded. "Maybe something's wrong with it. I mean, they clearly tried to send more."

"Why would it send only part of it?"

"It might've shorted out half way through and been done. Holding on by a thread." Clea tapped on her tablet for several moments. "I'm searching for any buoys that are reporting erratically or infrequently. This might get us closer."

"You could be right. But that might lead us into an ambush. Pirates like to pull that kind of nonsense."

"They do it so someone can't call for help," Clea pointed out. "The one we're looking for is actually broken. Besides, no one thinks to check the buoy before they go to their next location. And many civilians don't have scanners capable of such long range activity." One buoy began to blink nearly seven systems away. A *massive* jump.

If The Crystal Font made it all the way to such a remote location, they really went all out.

Durant may have been right about a second jump too. However, going so far seemed like a really bad idea unless they were directly pursued. Furthermore, if they really did jump twice, why go *deeper* into empty space?

Maybe it was all an accident. "I have to tell the captain," Clea said. "We need to investigate that location."

"You know, we might want to slow down a moment," Durant replied. "Why is the buoy damaged?"

"Age, perhaps. Who gets out there to maintain it?"

"Or environmental problems?" Durant shook his head. "The place might be flat out dangerous."

"We'll hop into the edge of space there," Clea said. "And perform our sensor sweep. If we find them, great but if not, we can fix that buoy while we figure out our next move. Believe me, someone would thank us in the future. If you got stranded out there without the ability to communicate, you'd be done."

"I hope you're right about this." Durant rose and moved to the door. "I'm going to finish my simulations with this new weapon. Let me know if you need anything from engineering."

"Will do." Clea grabbed her tablet and joined him. "With any luck, we'll be collecting our charge soon and heading back home. Maybe we can get away without having to fire the weapons again this mission but something tells me that would be too much to hope for, huh?"

"With this ship?" Durant laughed. "Yes, it would be far too much. See you soon."

***

Kale listened in on the tactical channel as both the ground force and air support coordinated together. The hot moment when those soldiers set down they were beset upon by enemy troops. The question of where they came from danced around in his mind and he knew Zanthari Varez was desperately seeking an answer.

Having replaced Deva on the bridge, the young man seemed a little nervous. Until that moment, he'd been working out of the tech labs. Sitting on the bridge for the alliance military could be intimidating, especially in the midst of a crisis. Listening to the fight over the speakers probably didn't help much either.

Thaina was running the action and Kale kept his mouth shut to let her. "What's happening now?" She asked, watching the cameras from the different soldiers. There was a slight delay in what she was seeing and what was actually happening. "Is everyone alright?"

"No," Lhar replied. "Bleise is dead. Yuris took a shot to the side but he'll survive. We've scanned one of these bodies and...well..."

"What is it, Vinthari?" Thaina insisted. Kale doubted the soldier needed pushing often. Whatever he saw must've really shook him up. "Report!"

"The enemy body disappeared. Deva believes it was made of pure energy."

"Contact!" Alma's voice exploded over the speakers. She led the air support that flew over the site. "Fighters incoming!"

"Fighters now again?" Kale shook his head. "They *must* have a base to be resourcing these things! Varez, have you found *anything* yet?"

Varez looked back at him helplessly. "I'm so sorry, sir. I just...there's nothing! No familiar energy readings, no hulls, no organics that match the enemy...They have to have some kind of new technology blocking them!" He yelped. "Sir! I think I know where they're coming from!"

"What?" Kale stood from his seat. "Show me."

Varez put an enemy capital ship up on the screen, coming from around the planet. It was one of their smaller warships, something that usually traveled in twos. Kale scowled as he took it in but didn't hesitate long. "Thaina, raise our shields and fire when ready. Full alert. Athan, get us moving. I want bombers out there right away."

As the bridge crew sprung into action, Kale couldn't help but think about the report suggesting the body might've been pure energy. Perhaps the enemy figured out a way to create lethal projections. It sounded far fetched but technology could do wondrous things. And these bastards were nothing if not industrious.

"They're closing to attack range," Athan said. "Thaina, that's all you."

"I'm on it." Thaina worked her console for several moments and their cannons began to fire, splashing into the enemy shields. "Direct hits. No appreciable damage. Their shields dropped to...eight percent and they're back on the rise."

Kale's com began to buzz and he slapped it as he sat back down. "What's going on up there?" Meira's voice sounded strained and exhausted. "Please tell me we're not in combat!"

"I'm afraid we've been attacked," Kale replied. "Enemy warship came from behind the planet. We finally know where the troops and fighters have come from. They've got some kind of base down there...perhaps even a colony."

"While that info is likely very important, I have some bad news. Extended fighting is *not* advisable. Not with our crystal in its current state."

"Suggestions," Kale replied firmly.

"Er...perhaps we can flee?"

"Without a power source to spark our new crystal, we'll be fleeing to nowhere. And they can chase us. Unless I'm very much mistaken, they seem fully functional." The ship shook from an enemy attack. Kale scowled and turned to Thaina. "Shield strength?"

"We're at ninety-percent. They...don't have the accuracy I'm used to. But we're not recharging as fast as I'd like."

"What can you do about that, Meira?" Kale asked.

Meira scoffed. "Pray? We're not in a condition to do much, Anthar!"

"Understood. Do what little you can to keep us alive and we'll do the same. Kale out." He clicked off his com and checked the damage reports. No one reported anything yet. He felt some anxiety slip away but not much. Meira was right. They didn't have a lot of fight in them, not with all the problems they were currently facing.

Thaina fired again, this time smacking the enemy right in the bow. Oddly enough, their attackers were still advancing on them. Kale got a bad feeling about proximity. He gestured to Athan, ordering him to put them in full reverse. "Give us some distance. They can't get too close. Where are our bombers?"

"They're launching now," Thaina said. "They were ready but the hangar's having some power issues. Apparently, our crystal fracture is causing more trouble than I would've guessed."

"We're at eighty-five percent energy output," Varez said. "So...I can see why we'd be having trouble."

"Just get them out there." Kale sighed. "And keep firing!"

"I'm on it!" Thaina fired again, this time a blast that wasn't quite at full power. She called out that the enemy's shields dropped to sixty-percent but they didn't even slow down. They counterattacked and their weapons were all direct hits. The lights flickered overhead but the shields held.

Probably just barely, Kale thought. *We have to finish this fight quickly and hope there aren't more of them. Where's your partner ship? You never go out alone.*

He wanted to ask Varez to keep scanning but knew it would be pointless. Perhaps their sensor equipment had been impacted in a way they didn't realize by the jump disaster or the crystal fracture. There were so few explanations for why they couldn't detect the people they were fighting. He wanted answers but first, they had to survive.

Fight first, investigation later.

***

Alma's wing engaged another squadron of enemy fighters, just moments after the ground crew claimed they secured the area. The ships came rocketing from around the back of the structure, their engines making a high pitched whine as they accelerated into action. Though six total enemies entered the fray, this time the Crystal Font pilots were not outnumbered.

The odds were even but they had to be conscious of where debris might land. If they fought directly over the operational zone below, they could jeopardize the soldiers trying to secure the power needed to get home. Alma ordered her people to draw the fighters away, even if they were only a kilometer off, it would make the whole situation safer.

Drawing back put them in a compromising position and they had to evade a wild amount of enemy cannon fire. Alma took a shot to the rear, her shields held and she climbed, entering into full dogfight mode. The others did the same, trying to spread the enemy thin as they worked into a steady combat rhythm.

Alma spun, her inertial dampeners screaming from the sudden motion. They didn't quite alleviate all the G force, especially in atmosphere and she strained against the urge to pass out. When the maneuver finished, she took several deep breaths, zeroing in on the target before her. Taking to the enemy's rear, her targeting computer got tone and she opened up.

Blasting the enemy with a full barrage, the ship didn't even try to evade. It took the attack, its shields burst and the fuselage ignited. A massive explosion resounded and fiery pieces plummeted to the ground below. Another *boom* caught Alma's attention to the left and she pulled up to rejoin the action.

Four enemies remained and they started to fly more as expected, climbing and dodging as the alliance pilots had seen through every battle in the past. This time, it proved much more difficult to get a firing solution and Alma cleanly missed the first couple shots. Another alliance ship screamed by, dropping a missile which chased its enemy into a canyon.

The ordinance caught the tail of the enemy just as he tried to pull away. The nudge sent him into a wall and his shields did nothing for the dramatic impact. As his core ignited, a huge chunk of the rock wall crumbled and fell, causing a massive dust plume to rise nearly two hundred feet into the air.

Two alliance ships teamed up on an enemy but it reversed its thrust, dropping behind them and firing. Alma tried to intercept but wasn't in time as a full spread struck one of her people, knocking their engines out. The pilot ejected just as the entire ship went up, more debris crashing into the ground.

Thank the Fates I moved us or the soldiers would be cursing our names right now.

Alma fired and though she missed, the enemies broke their formation and left the remaining alliance ship alone. Another pair of ally vessels joined her and let a spread of missiles go, chasing their targets down and blowing them out of the sky. Alma checked the scanner and saw only one left. He broke, heading back toward the structure.

They must *have a base back there!*

"Get him before he's over our companions," Alma said. "Everyone, chase him down." She opened her channel. "Search and rescue, we've got a pilot down. He ejected over the following coordinates." She fed them back to The Crystal Font as they rocketed after the final enemy, each of them taking shots, trying to lead him away from his destination.

All the ordinance proved too much for him to avoid and he began to spin as his shields went up. His burning vessel flew past the structure and a column of fire erupted from behind it, lasting for almost twenty seconds before black smoke replaced it. Alma flew to the wreckage, convinced she'd find an enemy base located below.

Instead, she only saw the smoldering remains of the fighter. Only trees spread out on the ground below. *This is getting beyond strange.* "Crystal Font, this is Vinthari Il'Var. We have defeated the enemy fighters. Area secured."

"Stand by," Thaina replied. "We're engaged with an enemy battleship up here. We might be calling you back but for now, maintain air superiority. You have to hold the area until we have that power. Understood?"

"Affirmative," Alma said. "Good luck."

Enemy battleship, Alma thought. *Where were they hiding? They had to be close by. Regardless, I suppose we know where they were this whole time and where they're coming from. If we take that out, we can expect to see no more action I suppose. Thank the Fates. I'd really like to get out of here soon.*

***

Lhar grabbed Deva, Vali and Niersa, pulling them aside from the main group. "The three of you need to get up those stairs and figure out if we can just walk in or not. Be careful. I don't want to lose more people on this world but we're going to have to take some risks."

"Will Yuris be okay?" Vali asked.

"Yes, when the shuttle gets here, we'll load him up and he can get out of here." Lhar checked his com and kicked a rock. "I just received a report that there's an enemy battleship up there fighting with the Font. That means Yuris has to hold on a little longer. I'll send Trias with you as well. The faster we finish our job, the quicker we can get home."

"Understood." Vali called over to Trias. "You're coming with us! Let's move out!"

"Where are we going?" Trias hurried over. "Up the stairs?"

Deva nodded. "The energy readings are coming from within there. But I can't tell if there's a door up there or not. If so, we're going to have to find a way in."

"I've got plenty of explosives," Niersa said. "In case we want to go in that way."

"I'm hoping we don't have to be destructive," Deva replied. "We might cause some kind of chain reaction. Let's treat this entire place as volatile until we know for a fact what we're getting into."

"Sounds good," Lhar said. "But move out! You're wasting time and we need you up there quickly." He moved over to Yuris and checked him over. The man was unconscious but his wound looked ghastly. The armor had melted into him, fusing with flesh and clothes. Physicians had their work cut out for them and that was if they got to him soon.

No basic first aid would cut it for this. The shuttle came back in for a landing and he determined to put his man on board then join the others. Gripping Yuris by the scruff of his armor, he dragged him over to the ramp and up. The copilot assisted him and they set the man down on one of the stretchers, securing him in place.

"Sir," the pilot's voice popped in his ear. "We've got contact moving on the stairs. Enemies seem to be pursuing our people."

"Where'd they come from?" Lhar asked. "Did you see?"

"Negative, sir. But there's five of them."

Lhar sighed and dismounted the ship, rushing toward the stairs. "Get back in the air," he ordered the shuttle then redirected his com. "Trias, you've got contact rear coming up the stairs. How far are you up?"

"Half way," Trias replied. "Whoa, there they are. We have no cover up here so we're going to keep moving. You in pursuit or should I open fire?"

"I'm only half way to the stairs. Fire until I say otherwise."

"Understood. Hope you get here quick."

Me too. Lhar broke into a sprint. *Me too.*

***

Deva stumbled up the stairs, struggling to maintain her footing as they rushed along toward the entrance above. From the air, the place appeared tall but as they tried to mount it, she got a much better perspective on its size. Some of the buildings back home were so large but they offered elevators rather than stairs.

Half way up, she panted like she'd been running half her life. Even with clean air from her suit, her lungs labored. Trias shoved her from behind and she collapsed on the stairs just as enemy weapons fire filled the air. *Another attack? Really? How?* Deva glanced back down and saw her companions open fire on their pursuers, five of them at least, who just arrived at the stairs.

Deva took aim but hesitated to fire. Her companions were in the way and she didn't want her first time pulling a trigger to result in a friendly casualty. She turned and began crawling her way up, peering at the daunting distance she had yet to cover. It might take her an hour to get up there on her hands and knees but at least she was able to catch her breath.

A pulse blast struck the stairs above her and she ducked until her the chin of her helmet tapped the stone beneath her. Cursing she glanced back again and saw there was at least one body near the bottom. Words burst into her ears but she couldn't process them, her mind was in a state of fight or flight.

When she finally calmed down, she realized she was hearing Lhar giving orders for them to spread out. He was about to flank the enemy and didn't want to get shot by one of his own. Trias grabbed Deva by the arm and yanked her hard to the left, dragging her to the edge of the stairs.

Alliance weapons fire rose above the noise of pulse weapons and the enemy started screaming, terrible, nightmarish noises Deva figured she would never forget for as long as she lived. How did they cry out so loudly? She shouldn't have been able to hear them from her vantage point so high above the valley floor.

Yet their deaths were felt by each of them. Lhar started up the stairs, shouting for them to move. Again, the enemy bodies began to disappear, disintegrating into thin air. *More of that strange projection thing that we talked about.* Deva wondered about it as she was pulled to her feet and compelled upwards. *The enemy must have found something hear to supplement their military.*

They arrived at the top with explosions going on overhead. The pilots were engaged with enemy fighters, dogfighting some kilometer off. Their engines tore through the sky, piercing the heavens with high pitch whines and sudden booms. Deva flinched after every sound, until she was practically crouching while they approached the massive portal leading inside.

Deva checked her scanner and frowned. A black door barred their path made of some stone material never cataloged by their science. An access panel sat to the left, aged and covered with dust. She approached and examined it, surprised to find it somehow familiar. *This couldn't possibly be our tech...*

A quick scan indicated the age to be *millions* of years but that sounded impossible. This was far too advanced for such a thing. She calibrated her sensors and tried again. Same results. Furthermore, her computer claimed their universal code should allow her to translate and use the terminal.

It can't be that easy! None of this can! What is going on?

"Contact!" Deva looked up as Trias shouted, firing to their right. Lhar joined her while Niersa and Vali watched their flank. Two enemies flopped on the ground, killed before they could get a shot off. Another one took cover and fired once before being shot in the face. "Get back on the console, Thi'Noch! Now!"

Deva cursed and returned to her duty, running the universal code and tapping her foot in anticipation. She watched, wondering exactly how long it would take but when it came back less than a minute with a full instruction set, she simply shook her head. *Thank the Fates this is all recorded because no one's going to believe me otherwise*.

"I'm in."

"What?" Lhar asked. "I didn't copy."

"I said I'm in!" Deva shouted. "I'll open it when you're ready."

"Stack up." Lhar gestured to the others and they took up positions on either side of the door, weapons aimed in. "Don't for a second think they aren't in there. Go, Deva. Open it!"

Deva held her breath and tapped the screen. Nothing happened immediately and she wondered if the translator made a mistake. A moment later the ground began to rumble beneath them as rock grated against rock. "I did it! It's opening! I got it!"

"Relax," Lhar snapped. "Stay back too. If they're in there, they'll certainly start shooting right away."

Deva noted that the energy readings increased noticeably as the door slid to the right. The spike might've been from the requirement to open but she didn't buy it. Something else was going on, something tapping into the power feed beyond a need to move a big old rock. Maybe the enemy was redoubling their efforts to get at them.

Possible. Their energy projections or whatever those are certainly would draw some power but why do they scream like they're dying? Is it some kind of virtual reality where the user feels the pain of their avatar? Movement distracted Deva from her thoughts and she watched the soldiers slip inside, gesturing for her to follow.

She stepped into the corridor, running another scan. *Nothing new! I thought for sure the outer wall would be causing interference. Sensors aren't getting anything new. This doesn't bode well for when we get to the source of power.*

The cavernous passageway extended some thousand yards ahead of them. Ten men could've walked abreast without touching the walls and the ceiling was bathed in shadow, making it impossible to tell how tall it was. A scan indicated more than fifty feet. Their footsteps echoed noisily even as they tried to be quiet.

"Deva," Lhar asked. "Do you have any lifeforms?"

"Negative...only us." Deva tapped her computer. "This seems impossible. The enemy *must* be down here!"

"They could be anywhere," Trias said. "Those things we killed out there weren't real. Probably from their ship."

"Which just seemed to show up." Deva hummed. "We better hurry. The source of power is coming from below us. There must be an elevator or more stairs."

"Pick up the pace." Lhar directed. "Double time it!"

Deva groaned internally at the thought of running. She was already exhausted. Picking up the pace made her legs complain and her back ache all the more. *When we get home, I'm requesting some serious leave time. This mission is undoing me.* The enemy might be waiting for them but she had to put the thought of her mind.

I have to focus on finding a way to transfer this power to the Font. Fates know they won't have an adapter down here.

***

Kale watched the report come in. Bombers were away and flying toward their objective. They would have a firing solution in moments and hopefully, their attack would slow the enemy down enough to buy some distance. Considering some of their previous tactics, they all knew that this particular enemy had no qualms about sacrificing vessels to take an objective.

And considering what they've been up to so far, I wouldn't be surprised if we were worth a quick kill.

The report from the surface about the bodies disappearing and the lack of wreckage on scans concerned him. Whatever technology they used couldn't have been developed in the short time the Crystal Font had been in limbo. This whole planet must've been a testing ground for it and Kale's crew just had the bad luck of stumbling on them.

Which would explain their interest in taking us out. If we got away, we could tell someone about what they have and then we might come up with a counter.

Kale figured his own government might consider sacrificing a battleship to save such a secret as projecting warriors on the battlefield. Risk nothing and gain an army. But if that were true, why did they show up in such small numbers? Why not project a hundred men and kill the landing crew? Why not fashion a thousand fighters and take down the pilots?

Limitations? Or maybe we're totally off base. What's another explanation?

Another direct hit shook the ship and Thaina cursed loudly. "Can you please perform those evasive maneuvers, Athan?"

"I'm not dancing over here," Athan grumbled back. "I'm trying. They're good shots!"

"Damage report," Kale said.

"Shields are at forty-five percent," Thaina said. "Bombers report they are ready to fire and are deploying their ordinance as we speak."

Kale crossed his fingers, silently praying to the Fates that this might give them the edge they so desperately needed. He tapped a button and brought the bombers up on his screen, their missiles streaking through space toward the enemy. There was no way they could avoid the attack, nothing they could really do but try to shoot them down.

But they didn't seem to even notice nor react. They continued firing at the Crystal Font, pressing forward with all the insistence of their suicidal companions from previous encounters. When the bombs hit, they flared brightly, causing the screen to compensate by falling dark. Thaina cried out for Athan to punch it.

The ship lurched as the shockwave hit them. All the lights went out and flickered back on a moment later. Thaina stood up, pointing at the screen. "They're gone! Look! They've been destroyed!"

Kale couldn't believe his eyes. He anticipated the bombs might've disabled them, or at least knocked out their shields. Perhaps slowed them down but obliterate them? Debris flickered around them for a few lingering moments before the chunks seemed to wink out of existence. One moment they were there, the next...they simply vanished.

"Did you just see that?" Athan asked.

"I did," Kale replied. "Thoughts?"

Varez shook his head. "I have no idea. What we just witnessed is physically impossible."

"We've been dealing with that a lot lately," Thaina added. "I think—"

"Anthar!" Varez interrupted. "I've got new readings!"

"Report. What are they?"

"Oh my...are you...no!" Varez slammed his fist into his console. "More enemy battleships!"

"Plural?" Thaina slumped in her seat and silence fell over the vessel. Kale knew why. If there were even two out there, they couldn't hold them back. There was no chance. Without the ability to jump or run, they would lose this fight. It was just a matter of time. "How many?"

"Four..." Varez swallowed hard. "Coming in fast."

All eyes fell on Kale. He didn't want to show them despair but he didn't have much positivity either. *I'm in a nightmare.* The sense of doom plunging down on them made his entire body ache but he didn't show any outward signs. He couldn't buckle, not now, not after everything they'd been through.

"Get ready," Kale spoke in a calm but firm voice. It was the best form of confidence he could convey. "This will be rough."

Chapter 7

Gray cross referenced the coordinates Clea provided with their star charts. She proposed they go well beyond any settled space, somewhere a buoy happened to be without a single colony anywhere nearby. None of the adjacent systems or even their neighbors had been colonized or frequented by anyone willing to report in.

Once they performed a jump into that space, they'd be on their own. He didn't anticipate finding The Crystal Font but they may well locate some pirates or other criminals hiding out. Those types might even have a base or colony all the way out there. Even with the bread crumb trail Clea followed, it began to feel like a true wild goose chase.

"You have our coordinates, Leonard?" Gray asked. "Edge of the system?"

"Yes, sir. Course laid in and ready." Leonard gestured to Redding. "You should see green."

"Jump is ready," Redding said, taking a deep breath. "Ready to engage."

"Do it." Gray gripped his seat as she hit her panel.

Space outside warbled for a brief moment and they winked into existence. Leonard and Olly sprung into action, tapping their consoles, pulling data from the surrounding area. Leonard called out confirmation that they'd arrived where intended. Olly announced he was scanning the system, pending a ping.

Gray felt like pacing but remained in his seat, giving his people a chance to work. Clea sat beside him, rigid as she waited as well. She and the tech crews worked feverishly on this assignment so every jump must've weighed heavily on them as they hoped their research paid off and didn't conclude with a buoy that had cleared its cache.

"The buoy seems to be online but I'm getting strange readings from it," Olly said. "Trying to get the message…wait! I've got ships! Multiple vessels!"

"What?" Gray stood up. "What do you mean?" How many?"

"Five," Olly replied. "Four Devaran battleships and…The Crystal Font! We found her!"

Gray felt a sense of relief and concern in equal measure. *Enemies? Out here? They must've traced them somehow but after so much time? This seems like the worst luck a captain could have.* "I trust they're in the middle of a fight then?"

"I'm reading problems with The Crystal Font's core," Olly said. "Some kind of power issue. They're not engaged yet but when they are..."

"They won't last long," Adam finished. "I'll get all pilots ready for launch. Should take less than five minutes."

"Leonard, get us a microjump course nearby," Gray ordered. "I want us in position to attack immediately."

Leonard frantically worked his controls, making the complex calculations required for such an endeavor. He'd gotten pretty good at it from their last few assignments. Not quite as proficient as his predecessor but certainly getting there. The young man probably never imagined a promotion to bridge staff would come so early in his career but he'd carried the responsibility well.

"Course ready." Leonard nodded to Redding. "Go for it."

"Weapons are hot," Redding said. "I'm good."

"Go."

They jumped again, this time the experience was far more jarring. Microjumps seemed to really hit hard but the ship especially complained after having just done so moments before. As they appeared nearby, Gray gestured to Agatha, having her reach out to the Crystal Font immediately. While he did so, engineering contacted him on his com.

Gray brought it up. "Atwell here."

"Captain, this is Durant. I hope you're not planning on pulling another jump in the very near future?"

"We'll see," Gray said. "There are four Devaran ships out there and we found The Crystal Font. Dedicate power to the weapons and hope. Atwell out."

"I've got the Font," Agatha said. "Putting on screen."

Kale Ru'Xin's face appeared, looking a little more exhausted than the last time they spoke but otherwise the same. "Captain Atwell," he said. "You have impeccable timing. We're in a bit of a mess here."

"We can see that." Gray nodded to Redding, gesturing for her to accelerate. "We're closing for battle. What's your situation?"

"We've already taken down one enemy vessel," Kale replied. "Then these four showed up and when I say that, I don't mean they jumped in. They literally appeared. Have you heard of some new technology where they can create energy projections of their forces?"

Gray shook his head. "No. Er...what do you mean?"

"We have a team on the planet and they encountered troops which disappeared when they died. Same with enemy fighters. If your tech officer scans the planet, he'll find a strange energy reading we've never seen before. It's off the charts. Unfortunately, we need it to spark our extra crystal so we can get out of here."

"I wondered. Have you been here all this time? Months?"

"No...a jump anomaly..." Kale paused. "I think we'll need to discuss this part after we survive."

"Agreed." Gray nodded. "We're launching fighters and are in position to open fire. Let's keep communication open for coordination."

"Agreed." Kale finally smiled. "Thank you for coming, Captain. We appreciate the help."

"Any time, Anthar." Gray motioned for Agatha to cut the screen. "Open fire when ready, Redding. Adam, ETA on fighter deployment?"

"Less than five minutes," Adam said. "Bombers are also ready. We'll have them deployed momentarily."

"Fantastic." *Alright, you bastards. Let's see how you like throwing down with a ship that isn't practically crippled.*

***

Wing Commander Meagan Pointer and her Panther wing launched from the Behemoth, preparing to escort a group of bombers. Once they cleared the ship, her eyes took in the objective and an involuntary gasp took her. Four battleships, grouped up and on rapid approach to The Crystal Font, powered up weapons for an assault.

What is so important out here in the middle of nowhere to warrant that kind of action?

"My God." Squadron Leader Mick Tauran muttered. "Where are their fighter screens? I'm not picking anything up on scans. Shouldn't they be trying to defend against what we're about to do?"

"I would've thought," Meagan replied. She clicked over to Wing Commander Rudy Hale's com. "Where are you? We're ready for an attack run."

"I'm out, waiting for the rest of the wing," Rudy replied. "We're going to have to be conservative with that many ships…hope for a chain reaction. I don't think we're going to have time for a reload in this fight."

"Probably not," Mick added. "And if they all launch their fighters, we don't have enough people to go toe to toe with them."

"Then let's make sure they don't have time to launch any," Meagan said. She accelerated to full speed, moving forward to scout ahead. *They must be jamming our scans somehow. There has to be fighters out there. Mick's right. Not even these animals would risk a bombing run unprotected*.

Even a little closer, she still didn't pick up anything on sensors. The ships were definitely powering up weapons, she could see their barrels burning red but they held their fire, allowing the Crystal Font to hammer them with cannon fire. The Behemoth let their weapons fly a moment later, pummeling the lead vessel.

Shields flared and she flinched as the forward defenses fell. Another barrage might cause some serious damage but if they could get their bombers in place, that might take one down completely. Even if the entire wing wasn't ready, the opportunity seemed like something they shouldn't waste.

"Rudy," Meagan said, "can you get someone over there to launch a couple bombs at that thing?"

"Yeah, I saw it too." Rudy sighed. "Get on my wing, Broussard. Let's take that thing down while the others assemble. We're going in!"

Meagan fell back to allow them to catch up. Even on afterburners they weren't as fast as the fighters. The massive ships lumbered up to her and continued on as two more Panther fighters fell in beside. The Behemoth fired another volley, this one tearing through the armor on the hull and ripping through key systems.

Orange-blue flames leaked out for a moment before some emergency system must've cut off the breach. Scans didn't indicate if the shields were up or not but they appeared to be. Even if they weren't, providing Rudy and his wing staggered their attacks, they should be able to cut through the defenses and tear them down, eliminating the threat.

"Twenty seconds to launch," Rudy said. "Are we sure there aren't any fighters out there?"

"Giant control," Meagan called out. "Do you have anything on scans? Fighters? Shields? My screens are practically coming back with nothing."

"I'll patch you through to the bridge," Revente sounded confused. "I don't trust what I'm seeing either."

Great, that's not a good sign. Meagan checked her chronometer and noted that Rudy and his partner would be firing any second. *It might not matter if you don't hurry, folks*.

"Uh...Panther One, this is the Behemoth," Olly's voice filled her cockpit. "I've got scans of their shields but no fighters. We have taken down their primary defenses. Another pass should disable the vessel. However, I do see you're with a couple bombers. We will redirect our attention to one of the other ships and let you finish that one off. Over."

"Thank you," Meagan said. "You heard him, Rudy. It's all yours."

Rudy fired first, three bombs that rocketed away from his ship and headed straight for the damaged cruiser. A count of ten saw the next volley off and all of their ships pulled away, hurrying back to their rally point from launching.

The computer suggested the estimated time to impact was less than thirty seconds.

We'll still be flying back to the others when they detonate. Meagan glanced over her shoulder just as the first three bombs struck the hull and exploded. The impact caused the battleship to list then various explosions pock marked the surface. Another three hit it on the belly, tearing through and creating a massive chain reaction.

The entire ship went up a second later, a bright flash filling space then going dark just as fast. Meagan checked her computer for the shockwave impact but nothing showed up. Frowning, she patched back over to Olly and asked him what happened. "What's the safe minimum distance? And did that explosion bother his buddies?"

"Um…" Olly sighed. "I have no idea what to tell you. There's no shockwave…no detonation to worry about…and the other ships seem completely unaffected despite their proximity. This makes absolutely no sense. Let me do some research but…well, it's not for me to say. I'm turning over any other orders to Commander Everly."

"Okay…" Meagan switched over to private com with Rudy. "You ever see anything like that?"

"Negative," Rudy replied. "Definitely new to me. Especially since we hit it with *six* bombs! Those alone should've caused some trouble. If not for them, then for us! I mean, they weren't all that far from the Behemoth but even our vessel didn't seem too troubled by that explosion."

"Olly said they're doing some research," Meagan said. "I think we're standing down for a moment."

"Sounds...good?" Rudy found a way to audibly shrug. "I don't know what to tell you. The rest of my wing's here. We're ready to attack."

"I've got something on scan," Mick interrupted. "Looks like they finally decided they need some fighters."

Of course they did. Meagan sighed. "Alright, get ready for intercept. I'll tell Giant Control and we'll do what needs doing. Rudy, you'd better hang back with the others and wait for us to cut you a decent path. Otherwise, this'll be a quick trip."

"Happy to let you lead the way," Rudy said. "Never much minded watching your behind."

"Cute." Meagan shook her head. "Panther wing, form up on me. Tiger, stay and protect the bombers. Giant Control, we're ready for intercept. Give the go word and we'll engage."

"Hang tight," Revente said. "We're not there yet but I'll give you the news momentarily. There's a lot of strangeness going on with these readings and I don't want to send you in without a better understanding of what's going on. Especially if we've just encountered a new kind of technology. Lord knows this won't be for the best."

***

Olly felt confounded. The readings and scans made no sense. How could they have absorbed the shockwave from the bombs and prevented the ships around them from experiencing the attack? Was it a new kind of containment to avoid blowing away a fleet when one ship went up?

Even so, he couldn't even imagine how such a technology would work. A safety protocol for total break down of the core? Not from the type of trauma they were put through. But he had no good explanation for what he'd seen. The readings he received didn't help. Nothing really explained the event and no matter what program he put the data through, it all came back the same.

Unexplainable.

Olly patched into The Crystal Font and got their secondary tech officer, Varez on the line. He posed the problem to him, hoping the kielans may have already determined their enemy's advantages. Unfortunately, they were just as confounded. Whatever strange power came from the planet *must* have something to do with the enemy's newfound abilities.

And that might mean they've designed some kind of new power unit to do God knows what. Apparently, anything. But I don't buy it. They would've employed all this by now. We would've heard about it, encountered it during a fight. Not found it in some remote place that The Crystal Font just happened upon.

"Captain, I don't know what we're seeing," Olly reported, "but it's beyond unnatural. Even the Font doesn't quite understand and they've been here a while. Apparently, the fighters on the surface did the same and bodies are disappearing. If that battleship somehow did the same thing…and more importantly, where did our bombs go? If they detonated, there should've been some kind of feedback but they just winked out too."

"Any theories at all?" Gray asked. "Clea? Olly?"

"They have created a projection device," Clea said, "capable of creating carbon copies of themselves and their vehicles which in turn can fight and cause real damage."

"That's a theory?" Adam smirked. "Sounds like fact the way you put it."

Clea shrugged. "It's one possibility but certainly not the only one. Olly, do you have any thoughts?"

Olly's mouth dropped open and he shook his head helplessly for a moment. "I...don't really know. I...I mean, the project ideas sound...it might explain the latency in their attacks. They're not nearly as quick as we're used to. They didn't even have fighters out there a few minutes ago and now, they do. *After* we took out their first battleship."

"And four more showed up," Gray said, "after The Crystal Font dealt with one of their cruisers."

"Interesting how that's working out," Redding said. "Like they're not sure how much power to use to take us out?"

"If it's even them," Agatha said. All eyes fell on the communications officer and she blushed. "What I mean is, maybe the enemy isn't responsible for all this? It could be something to do with the planet instead."

"How?" Olly asked.

"I don't know that," Agatha replied. "I was just offering a theory."

"A good one," Gray added. "After all, we can't assume the enemy's involved in this. They might be but if they're not, we need to be looking elsewhere. What made you think of that, Agatha?"

"I tried to pick up their communications," Agatha answered, "but there's no radio communication between the vessels at all. Not even coded. In fact, I read only one mappable frequency and that seems to be an energy source. No shields, no chatter and no interference from their mass. Nothing."

"Wait, energy source?" Olly turned back to his console and tapped away. "Can you feed it over?"

"It's sent."

Olly really focused for a moment as the cannons fired again. They were struck by a blast but he ignored the rattling and shaking, drawing more data from the surrounding area. He had an exact duplicate of what Agatha found and it was from the energy source on the planet. As he put them on top of one another, he confirmed that they were, indeed, the same.

Either the enemy is on the planet or the planet is the enemy. Olly relayed his opinion to the bridge crew and none of them spoke for a moment. Clea joined him, checking his findings and scrutinizing the data. She nodded once and confirmed what he suggested. "I agree. These ships are directly related to the planet somehow."

"We need to establish some facts," Gray said. "Right away. Clea, I want you on that. Olly, focus on the battle. We need scans of the ships during the fight. How's the Font doing?"

"They've taken a bit of a beating," Olly said. "But they're doing okay. Shields holding but hull took a licking in the last barrage. Enemy fighters are ready to engage our people. I'm recommending we take them down so the bombers can work some magic. Can we send them in?"

"I'm on it," Adam said. "Keep hammering away at them Redding."

"They're moving closer to the Font," Olly said.

"Intercept," Gray ordered. "Redding, do *not* let that ship get up on them. Focus all firepower on them right now. I didn't come all the way out here to lose our allies now and they certainly didn't survive so long just to die in a senseless battle in the middle of nowhere. Keep efficient but let's make things a little faster, folks. For all our sakes."

***

Meagan had plenty of experience battling enemy fighters. She'd flown countless simulations and then engaged them multiple times in the last several months. Their style and tactics were well known to her. They tended to fly in groups of three, covering each other throughout a fight and maneuvering in unpredictable ways.

This meant taking one of them down could be a serious challenge. Meagan's people proved highly successful against them before they upgraded their inertial dampeners. Engaging them now meant making full use of their new advantage and she thought it might be necessary since they would be dramatically out numbered.

So when she shot down her seventh fighter in less than five minutes, Meagan knew something was seriously wrong.

Yes, the enemy flew wildly and took shots at them but they didn't seem to be really trying.

They lacked whatever passion drove them on in a serious conflict and though they had several close calls, none of the Behemoth fighters had even been damaged yet. *Either we've gotten really good or they fielded their C team.*

A moment after the thought crossed her mind, one of her opponents attempted to collide with her and as she banked away from him, he slammed into his own wingman. The two enemy vessels exploded and winked out of existence, simply gone. Meagan didn't have time to really think about it and kept her head in the game, acquiring a firing solution on her next target.

"Anyone wonder why this isn't a little harder?" Lieutenant Kelly Parson, Panther Seven, asked. "I've got nine kills already."

"Right there with you," Lieutenant Paris Tullefson flying in Panther Five, replied. "They're shooting but not nearly as often or heavily as they do in simulation...or back at the research facility."

Mick responded, "won't matter if we can't whittle their numbers down. Scans indicate they brought in reinforcements. Another twenty!"

"Twenty?" Meagan groaned. "And I thought I was doing well over here. I would've sworn they'd have launched everything by now!"

A missile flew by her, nearly connecting with Mick's ship. He managed to avoid it but the projectile started chasing him. He hit the afterburners and Meagan closed behind him, acquiring a firing solution and letting the computer get tone. As it buzzed, she fired a short burst and ordered him to climb.

Her shots took out the missile and would've smacked him in the tail had he not gotten out of the way.

"Thanks," Mick said. "I would've thought he'd have followed that up though."

"Something's wrong. This feels like..." Meagan paused. "Like an easy simulation."

"Those missiles sure seem real enough," Paris said.

"And I took a shot from one of their pulse cannons," Kelly added. "Sure didn't feel like a simulation to me. I've got minimal damage by the way."

Meagan admired her scans for a moment, disengaging from combat. Oddly enough, no enemy fighter pursued her. As she left the fight and climbed out of the general chaos, she pinged the enemy battleships and tried to get an accurate count of the fighters flying around. Her computer showed blips but they faded in and out, some vanishing entirely.

I hope the Behemoth's on this because I have no clue what that means. Meagan noticed a couple of enemy ships trying to close on one of tiger wing's tails so she flew down to assist, firing missiles just as she got into range. One of them went down in an instant and the other broke away, fleeing the attack. *At least they sometimes seem worried about dying.*

Another battleship exploded, the one closest to The Crystal Font. As the light brightened space around them, Meagan winced. *I hope the shockwave doesn't damage them even worse.* But when the core finished, the ship was simply gone. No wreckage, no hull, no burning debris. Like everything else, it simply ceased to be.

"Did you see that, Mick?"

"Kinda busy!" Mick yelled back. "In fact, I could really use some help over here!"

"My bad. I'll be right there." Meagan twisted her controls and engaged in the fight again, taking her mind off the high level problem and focusing. She rocketed closer, just in time to watch a blast of cannons cause Mick's shields to flare.

Pulling the trigger, she perforated one of the enemy ships, tearing through its shields and littering the cockpit with weapons fire. That craft spun out of control and went spiraling toward the planet. She redirected her attention to the other one who pulled an outrageous maneuver, practically flipping in place to take some shots back at her.

Meagan disengaged, diving to avoid the attack and hitting her afterburners to gain some speed but the enemy remained tight on her tail. Going full evasive, she veered around his shots, narrowly avoiding a full blast several times, even as grazes caught her shields and nudged her with their impact.

"Need some help!" Meagan called into the com. "Anyone available?"

"I've got it," Flight Lieutenant David Benning said. He flew in Panther Three. "Mick's a little busy, I stepped in for him. Please bank left, ma'am."

Meagan felt a hint of annoyance at how casual he sounded but she complied, moving the direction he requested. When nothing immediately happened, she wondered what he was doing but just as she decided to say something, an explosion behind her explained. The enemy blip disappeared from her scanner.

They formed up together and headed back toward the main fight. "Thanks," Meagan said. "Appreciate the assist."

"No problem. Looks like they launched another ten."

"They have to run out some time," Meagan replied. "Listen up, Panther. We're putting in some overtime on this one but if you need to reload, let us know and get back to the ship. They're prepared for hot transfers. Just don't let yourself run out completely. Getting back won't be fun. But as we're in for the long haul, good luck and keep reporting in. We've got this."

***

Gray watched the first battleship go up, leaving three behind. *They were barely putting up a fight. I bet that one was going for a self destruct. I wish I could say this was predictable behavior but in this case, they're hardly putting up a fight. Even in numbers, they have to actually use their weapons to win. What's going on?*

As if to answer his question, all three enemy cruisers opened up, firing volleys of cannon fire. Shields flared on their ship and he noticed The Crystal Font was experiencing the same fate. He frowned, wondering what suddenly changed. *Why didn't they do this* before *we took down their companion?*

"Olly," Gray leaned forward. "Try Protocol Seven on target number three. The one on the starboard side. Redding, target and fire on his mark."

"Sir?" Olly glanced over his shoulder. "We…we know it doesn't work anymore."

"Try it anyway." Gray shrugged. "What's it matter either way?"

"Okay…" Olly began tapping away. "Shields holding at eighty percent but they're really pounding us…too heavily in fact. I thought they had to refresh their weapons more often."

A moment later the enemy barrage ended.

"Weird…they're recharging." Olly shook his head. "Protocol Seven ready. I'm sending it now." He watched his scanner and his eyes widened, jaw dropping. "It…worked! Redding, fire!"

Redding opened up, letting everything they had go. She coordinated with The Crystal Font who also gave them a full blast from their cannons as well. The combined force against an unshielded ship caused catastrophic damage. Massive explosions marred the hull and the core went up in a spectacular light show.

But the ships nearby didn't so much as have their shields flare up and the Behemoth didn't feel any shockwave from the destruction.

"I have a feeling that won't work again," Gray said. "Though you're welcome to try on the next ship."

"Why wouldn't it work?" Adam asked. "That thing couldn't have transmitted information to its buddies. These ships must've been off the network for so long they didn't get any update about our weapons."

Gray shrugged. "A hunch. I'm starting to piece together the puzzle but it's still the same damn color. Agatha, how's the buoy? Can we get a message out?"

"There are people performing maintenance," Agatha said, "still working through it despite what's going on. It needed serious maintenance and they took it offline to do so. We can't send anything yet."

"Fantastic," Gray muttered. "Keep checking. The second they get it back so we can call for help."

"Sir," Olly said, "I've got another *six* enemy battleships incoming and they're leading with their best foot. They're opening fire!"

"I hope Clea figures this out soon." Gray stood up. "The odds just got terrible. Agatha, work with The Crystal Font on an evacuation plan. If we can get them over here, we can jump out of here and avoid further conflict. Make it fast and efficient. We can't handle the odds if they continue to multiply like this."

***

Clea joined Paul in the tech lab and used several of the computers to run simulations, trying to identify the signal and see what exactly it was doing. The planet seemed to be emanating more power than it had when they initially arrived. Comparing it to what The Crystal Font sent them upon their arrival, it had been pumping out only a low level of energy then.

Something's pushing it now. Some kind of operation. If the enemy's down there, they must be using more and more to fight us off.

Tapping the com, Clea brought up The Crystal Font. "This is Tathin An'Tufal of the Behemoth. I need to contact your ground crew on the surface. Can you please give me the frequency?"

"This is Zanthari Wena Fi'Devo," the response came back, "and yes, I'm sending it over now, ma'am. Please let me know if there's anything else I can do."

"Thank you." Clea sat back in her chair and turned to Paul. "Keep monitoring the signal and check whether or not it is somehow being cast into space or if it's localized. At first I thought it might be surrounding the world only but maybe I was wrong. The sheer magnitude of it is overwhelming our sensors so we might have to take down the fine tuning."

"I'm on it." Paul worked quickly but it would still take a few moments. Clea sat back and waited to connect up with the ground forces. Their perspective might well answer a lot of questions. Depending on how dangerous it was down there and what they were facing. As the ship shook from an incoming attack, the urgency of the situation amplified.

Sorry, Gray. I'm going as fast as I can.

***

Deva and the others arrived at what her scanner suggested was an elevator. Another panel blocked their way but once again, the universal code got her in quickly enough. She tapped away and the doors opened, this time with far less noise than the front area. As they stepped inside, she marveled at how massive it was, once again nearly fifty feet high and vast in each direction.

They must've hauled some serious gear down here. Deva turned to the panel. *They couldn't have been giants or that would be a lot bigger...and higher.*

The elevator began to move but it was subtle enough that they could only tell by the tiniest vibration in their feet. Lhar and the others took the best cover they could and held their weapons at the door. Deva moved behind them, aiming her weapon toward the floor with her finger off the trigger.

This thing is a last resort.

"Deva." Wena's voice in her helmet made her jump. "Do you copy?"

"I'm here," Deva muttered irritably. "I'm a little busy down here. What's going on?"

"I'm patching in Tathin Clea An'Tufal from the Behemoth. She needs to talk to you urgently."

"Oh! Wait, the Behemoth's here?" Hope gripped her heart and she felt a sense of excitement rise in her. "That's fantastic news! Patch her through! Quickly!"

"Did you just say the Behemoth's here?" Lhar asked. "And how far are we going down anyway?"

"They're here," Deva nodded. "Give me a moment."

The connection established and Clea spoke first. "Hello, Vinthari. We don't have a lot of time so forgive my lack of greeting. I need a better understanding of what you're finding down there. Do you have any more data about the energy readings we're picking up? Do you know what's causing it? What's creating it?"

"I have some information," Deva said. "I've scanned one of the bodies we killed that disappeared and it proved to be pure energy. No organic material whatsoever. Furthermore, the energy has been increasing as we've pressed closer to the core. Whatever's controlling it might be working harder to protect whatever we're about to find."

"Understood. We're finding a similar pattern with the battleships up here."

"Wait, battleships? As in more than one?" Deva swallowed hard. "How many?"

"Eight right now," Clea replied, "which seems rather impossible. However, they are causing damage when they shoot and our ordinance is definitely hitting something when we fire back. We need to know what they are and how they've been made. The key *must* be down there where you're going."

"I agree...and we're getting closer." Deva checked her scanner. "We're on an elevator going deep into the planet. I'm guessing the power source isn't the core of the world itself but it might have access to it."

"Let me know the moment you find something."

Lhar immediately began questioning Deva and she did her best to answer his questions but they primarily revolved around the attacking forces. He believed if they could leverage the kind of numbers against them that those starships represented, they could land a number of troops and outnumber them with ease.

In fact, he expressed confusion as to why they hadn't done it yet.

"If this facility belongs to them, they should've already taken us down," Lhar said.

"We have killed quite a few," Trias said. "Maybe they didn't have that many people down here to begin with."

Deva allowed the military people to talk about the odds and numbers, devoting her attention to her scanner. The power output had increased considerably and as they got closer, she realized that they were standing on more directed energy than she might've measured in six battleship engine cores.

This place could take care of the entire capital back home without running out. Clean power forever.

The elevator slowed down and stopped, bringing her back to the moment. Stress gripped her as the soldiers aimed their weapons at the door. Deva took up a position between Trias and Lhar, pointing her gun outward as well. She kept her finger off the trigger, to prevent a mishap but knew the second the door opened, she might need to fire.

This is the moment of truth. If this place is protected, we may well not survive the next sixty seconds. Fates, I hope you didn't lure us down here only to die. We're too close to escape. The door began to open and she held her breath. Here we go.

***

Chapter 8

Gray gripped his seat as the ship shook violently, a reaction to a series of blasts from several enemy vessels. Shields held but he knew they wouldn't last long. Not under that punishment. Worse, there was nothing he could do to make any of their plans move faster and everyone was already doing their jobs.

Evacuating The Crystal Font would take time and they'd have to risk a lot of people trying to make the trip over to the Behemoth. This wouldn't allow them to save those on the surface either. With eight enemy warships, they technically should've cut bait and run but Gray couldn't do it. Not when they came so close to their objective.

At a certain point, I'll have to do so. If only to get some backup out here and stop the enemy from whatever they're doing.

A flash on the screen caught his attention. Two of the enemy went up, exploding in a spectacular burst of light. He took a deep breath, unable to feel much enthusiasm for their success. Two down, six to go didn't mean much in this situation. He turned to his tablet, checking for reports but nothing new had come in.

Adam leaned close, keeping his voice low. "Our pilots report additional units are joining the fray. Our bombers are returning for reload. It's getting worse."

"Sure isn't getting better," Gray replied. "We have to buy time...for us and them."

"You might've already thought about this," Adam said, "but we should seriously consider jumping out of here. Get some reinforcements and come back. The buoy won't be back online in time to help us. There's no point in dying out here. It won't serve anyone."

"Yes, I've thought about it. But I'm not ready to give up. When it looks like we've got no other choice..." Gray stood up and moved to Leonard. "Plot a course out of this system. Get us some good jump coordinates. We need to be prepared."

"I'm on it."

Gray heard the hesitation in the young man's voice. He didn't want to leave. Taking off at that point would mean they failed, that they lost the people they were there to save. Adam's practicality might've been the right thing to do but it certainly didn't feel like it. Another volley splashed against their shields.

The ship trembled and Gray grabbed Leonard's chair to stay on his feet. "Shields?"

"Fifty percent," Olly said. "Though honestly, I don't know how we're doing so well. Their weapons should be doing a lot more damage."

Gray agreed. The ridiculous odds would've been more than enough to take out both vessels, even if The Crystal Font had been fully functional. The puzzle became more complex and Clea needed to provide the key to solving it. Maybe they'd figure it out in time to save everyone but confidence began to slip.

***

Lhar opened fire, executing two enemy soldiers waiting outside the door. The hallway narrowed in comparison to the one above and the ceiling was barely twelve feet high. The doors didn't open as much as they could, just enough to allow them to depart. They'd have to step over the bodies to get in.

"Is this the only other floor?" Lhar asked.

"No…" Deva said. "Yes?" She checked the panel again. "Okay, there are others but they seem to be maintenance corridors. Shorter…they might not even big enough for one of us to get through. I tried to get us as close to the power reading as possible. The core of this place. My scans say we're close. The end of the hallway, there's a room. We have to get there."

"Your scans show any more enemies?" Trias asked. "Mine's coming up empty."

"No," Deva said. "Nothing but the core. Can we go?"

Lhar sighed. "Dying doesn't make us faster. Trias, you and I are on point. The rest of you are with Deva. Let's go."

He dashed forward, keeping his weapon in front of him. If someone came out at the end, they'd be helpless. He had to be prepared to fire, to take a head off if one peeked out. The walls seemed to close in on him as he moved along, the narrow corridor proving to be a dramatic contrast to the one they'd entered through.

A silhouette appeared and he pulled the trigger, the stock of his gun biting into his shoulder. Something screamed, their voice echoing off the ceiling. Trias tapped his arm, taking his place in the lead. Lhar hoped Deva could figure out what they needed when they got to the end but despair threatened to overwhelm him.

Even if they figured out how to tap the energy, it wouldn't necessarily matter. They couldn't swap out the crystal in the middle of a space battle and if there were more than one of them out there...the mission they were risking their lives for meant nothing. Success, failure, life, death, all came to the same end.

As they reached the second doorway, the elevator closed down the hall. Trias cried out, aiming her weapon in that direction. "Are we trapped?"

"No," Deva replied. "The panels were working just fine."

"Why'd it close then?" Lhar asked.

"Maybe...someone else summoned it?" Deva shrugged. "Elevators close on their own back home? I don't know!"

Trias grabbed her arm. "You really need to start putting some pieces together. We're putting our lives on the line on *your* word!"

"Settle down," Lhar ordered. He peered through the door, ignoring the fact that the body he'd shot on the way down had already disappeared. Lights burst to light overhead and he fell back taking aim. *You're getting twitchy*, he thought. *Relax.* "Is this where we want to be?"

Deva stepped past him into a room roughly twenty by twenty. The walls appeared smooth like polished stone and there were no other exits. Illumination came from panels overhead, each glowing sky blue. The soldiers stepped inside and took position around the door, and Lhar left them to guard it as he followed the tech officer.

"Now we know the enemy's pulling some kind of technological marvel," Lhar said. "That guy I shot had no where to come from unless he was already in here."

"We knew they were using a marvel when they disappeared," Deva replied, tapping her computer. "The walls are monitors I think. We've come to some kind of control room."

Lhar grumbled. "How do you know?"

"I'm getting the same readings I did from the panel by the elevator." She hit a button and the wall opposite the door burst to life, showing a variety of messages in some foreign language. Lhar marveled at it for a moment but looked away, peering over the rest of the room. "Yes! I can access this!"

"Um…" Trias drew his attention to the door. "Looks like the elevator's opening again."

"Great." Lhar grumbled. "Can you close this up? At least partially?"

"I'll try," Deva said. "I need to communicate with Tathin An'Tufal as well. We can figure this out, Lhar! We'll get out of this. I promise!"

Lhar didn't have the heart to tell her his opinion. He figured he'd rather go out fighting regardless but her enthusiasm, her naivety, knotted his stomach. If she came to the same realization he had, she might well give up. They may well be facing the last moments of their lives anyway. He didn't see any reason to spend them in useless despair.

"Then hurry up." He aimed down the site of his weapon, waiting for the first person to step out in the open. "Times wasting as they say."

***

Clea watched the feed from Deva, desperate to do more than watch but helpless at the moment. The transmission showed they arrived in a control room, some kind of central nervous system for the complex probably. If so, it may well be the way to manipulate the power source The Crystal Font sent them for.

But how exactly could they tap it for sparking their crystal? There didn't appear to be any way to plug in to the thing. *Maybe they need to get those monitors on and tell the computer to transfer some energy to a portable device. If my calculations are right, they won't need much but an engineer should definitely take a look.*

She sent a quick message to Durant, providing him the information she had. He'd be able to give them an accurate and quick response on what they needed. Of course, both he and the engineer aboard The Crystal Font were likely busy trying to keep them alive. The Behemoth was holding its own but for how long?

I wonder if Gray's thinking about leaving. Two ships could not be lost out there. It didn't feel particularly heroic but she understood the notion. *Deva has to hurry.* The camera feed was delayed by a few moments so when a monitor burst to life, Clea figured it must've been on for a good five seconds.

"What did you discover?" Clea asked. Voice was real time.

"I've tapped into the computer network of the complex," Deva replied. "I'm analyzing it now and sending back the data as I record it. I...think I understand what's going on and more importantly, I can confirm that the enemy is *not* present here. Take a look at this. Please confirm my conclusion."

Clea watched as translated data filled her screen. She gestured for Paul to join her but he needed to go to his own terminal and translate the kielan language. Whoever built the complex left behind instructions on how to utilize their facility, a help file for lack of a better term. They wanted someone to come along and use it.

But why are we under such heavy attack then?

"Contact!" Lhar shouted. "From the elevator!"

Gunfire erupted over the com and Clea had to turn it down. She read quickly, doing her best to ignore the action. *Deva must be stressed beyond belief.* After the research facility, Clea knew how frightening field operations could be. Yet she left the ship another time while they pursued the recorder from her previous ship.

One does what they have to.

Paul broke her thoughts, "this is fascinating! I can't believe we found such a thing."

I only hope our discover will be something we can share.

***

Meagan fought exhaustion and pain lancing through her muscles. The constant dogfighting was wearing her down and she knew she wouldn't last much longer. Two of their ships had been disabled but not destroyed. There was no explanation. The enemy simply stopped shooting at them.

The bombers had to return to be reloaded and hadn't returned yet. Panther wing likely needed to do the same with their missiles. As Meagan dodged an enemy that tried to collide with her, she fired a burst on another one and took him out. Flying through the explosion, she had to spin to the left to avoid another attack and hit her afterburners to get out of a particularly nasty brawl.

Mick called out to her, asking for her position. She told the computer to send it to him, focusing on her flying instead. They'd link up again and work together. Everyone got separated for a short period of time. The action out there made the craziest simulation look like easy mode. There were so many enemy fighters, they practically didn't have to aim.

Another fighter on Tiger wing went down, disabled. Two bomber wings reported they were back on the field and heading for their targets, more of the battleships. They'd proved to be fairly easy to take down and Meagan risked a chance to count them. They were down to five. Considering the odds, she couldn't believe they'd been so successful.

This will definitely go down as our most bizarre engagement to date.

Three enemies got on her tail and she groaned, performing a dive. Mick let her know he was on them, scattering the enemies and giving her some breathing room. She pulled a wild maneuver, spinning to get a shot off on them and her left shoulder flared up, shooting pain down her back. *Not the time!*

Pulling the trigger, she ended another one. If not for the computer, Meagan would've lost track of how many she shot down. Mick took out the other two and they formed up, prepared for the next wave. *How long can this possibly go on? Why are they not experiencing any fatigue at all? It's not like this is easy on them.*

"You're all about to have a worse day," Revente said. "Reinforcements are incoming."

"Are you kidding me?" Meagan clenched her fist in frustration. "Thanks, great news. We're on it."

"Captain's about to order you to withdraw," Revente replied. "Start working your way to a position to disengage. All ships, prepare to disengage. Bombers will deploy your payloads and head back. Acknowledge."

"Acknowledged," Meagan replied. *They mean to jump out of this sector...without The Crystal Font. We'll have come out here for nothing. And we won't be able to get our disabled pilots either. This is a cluster.* "You heard them, Mick. Start falling back." *Even if it is going to stick in my craw for a long time.*

***

Kale checked the statistics of his fighters and noted that they were doing quite well despite the sheer numbers out there. Shields were holding on The Crystal Font as well, a miracle worked by

Meira for sure. His people worked hard to survive against overwhelming odds, odds which would certainly end them eventually.

Deva's report suggested they made it to the control center of the facility they located. Unfortunately, the soldiers were once again engaged with enemy ground forces. Kale already knew the result of their mission. Even if she found the power source, they couldn't spark the crystal and replace it while under attack.

The second the crystal left the assembly, they'd be down to environmental shields only. Weapons would tear through that in seconds. Furthermore, the Behemoth wouldn't be able to stay for much longer. They couldn't risk being destroyed out there. He knew they were on the verge of abandonment and he didn't blame them at all.

We don't both have to die.

The fact they were down to five battleships out there shocked him as well.

Thaina clapped her hands. "Direct hit!" Kale looked at what she was talking about and noted she'd managed to get their weapons through an enemy's shields and cause their core to overload.

They hadn't blown up yet, but the reaction was obvious on their scanners. That ship was done.

"Fantastic work." Kale's heart wanted to start hoping but practicality beat it down. Knocking them down to four meant they'd already done the impossible. Bombers from both sides were engaging again, preparing to fire at the remaining ships. They might even take two down. If that was the case, then the Behemoth just might be able to finish the rest off.

Fighters wouldn't be as hard without a base.

I can't say anything but this just might work.

The entire ship shook as if to dash Kale's hope. "Report!"

Varez held on to his console and shouted back, "bomb hit us! Shields are at twenty percent!"

Kale slapped his own console. "Meira! Can you get us more power?"

"The crystal fractured again," Meira replied. "I'll do what I can but if we're being honest, this thing has *maybe* ten minutes of combat left in her. Conservatively, I'd assume five."

Five minutes. This ship will be lost in a matter of minutes. "Understood. Do what you can!

The battle's going far better than it should. Squeeze whatever you can out of that thing."

"On it, sir."

"Did we get the bomber dealt with, Thaina?"

Thaina nodded. "Turrets took the others down before they could release their payloads. We were very lucky."

"That seems to be going around." Kale narrowed his eyes. He'd studied space combat extensively and yes, a few battles had seemed to embody the definition of fortune. Most came down to simple tactics and numbers. Whether they lived or not, if someone reported on what happened, it would go down in the history books.

If anyone's ever allowed to talk about it. "We don't have a lot of time, Thaina," Kale said. "Make it count." He turned to Deva's report and started to read, hoping for some good news.

***

Deva glanced over her shoulder and wished she hadn't. She couldn't even count the number of enemies in the hallway but the bastards had no cover. Lhar and his people cut them down easily, tearing through their ranks with quick bursts.

However, she knew they'd run out of ammo soon. Then it wouldn't matter how easy they were to shoot.

Turning back to the screen, she began reading the greeting.

Welcome, visitor! Thank you for visiting the V'ka'lin Sanctuary. This state of the art facility was designed for study, learning and leisure. All root species have been considered for as designers, we know our labors in the far off parts of the galaxy will eventually leave their systems and travel the stars, just as we did so long ago.

This facility and everything in it has been designed to ensure our visitors are able to function and survive on the surface. Please note that hostile action against other living beings will result in disablement. We have a glorious safety record in regards to public order and companionship. It would be a shame to lose our rating over a simple misunderstanding.

"This is crazy..." Deva muttered into her com. "Are you seeing this, Miss An'Tufal?"

"I am," Clea replied. "The rest seem to be regulations for the facility. Try to click through so we can find the exact purpose or even better yet, a menu."

Deva tapped her own screen, interfaced directly with the machine. A moment later, she saw a menu appear with six options. The terminal had to translate them and she tapped her foot, anxiety compelling her to motion. Behind her, the conflict raged on. She dared a look and the numbers did not seem to diminish at all.

"I'm out!" Trias shouted, switching to her side arm. Deva hurried over and gave her a magazine and set her rifle down beside them. "I'm good again!"

"Keep it up," Lhar said. "But be as conservative as you can with what you've got."

Deva hurried back to the terminal and swallowed hard. *Maybe I should close the door*. She didn't think the enemies could get in. Not for a long while. Of course, what would happen when they had to leave? She'd give Lhar and his people a chance to tell her when to do so and instead focus on the task at hand.

The menu finished translating and Deva squinted up at it. Despite the size, the words were hard to make out against a dark blue background. The font was an off white color, with the top box flashing. An animated background made it all the more confusing as yellow lines pulsed in various, seemingly random directions.

Status. Power Core. Relays. Planetary Alignment. Log Files. Messages.

Deva tapped the power core button and a wall of technical data appeared. Her computer translated that much quicker as it didn't seem to be an embedded graphic. It expressed that the energy supply was operating at eighty-eight percent efficiency and with a little maintenance could be back to ninety-nine in short order.

Apparently, the relays needed adjustment but all things considered, Deva figured they didn't need to worry about that yet.

"Show me the log files," Clea said. "Wait! Check *status*. I would've assumed what we just read fell under that option so this will be interesting."

Deva complied, tilting her head as a message sprawled across the screen.

All projectors are online and functioning normally. Scanning thoughts…worry. Fear. Terror. Adjusting accordingly.

"What's that mean?" Deva hummed.

"Log files now," Clea said. "Hurry."

Deva tapped those instead and stepped back as another wall of text displayed.

Situation One: worry about the enemy they are warring with. Calculating...War Class Fighter Devaran Ilatha. Forming and deploying.

Situation Two: Ilatha not performing as expected. Calculating...adjusting tactics based on known behavior.

Situation Three: wondering where the enemy might be coming from. Advanced culture. They have blocked all thoughts of the simulation for immersion. Calculating...deploying Devaran War Band.

Situation Four: continued concern about source of enemy. Poor rating expected for experience. Calculating...deploying Devaran battleship.

Situation Five: skepticism. Poor rating guaranteed. Calculating...deploying additional Devaran battleships.

Situation Six: arrival. New space vessel has entered system. Odds have turned. Calculating...deploy more forces.

Ground...deployed. Air...deployed. Space...deployed. Double them to provide challenge.

Situation Seven: prepare survey for opinion results. Offer apologies for the slow turn around of many services. Apologize for not creating accurate simulation.

"This is a game!" Deva shook her head. "The enemy wasn't projecting...this *thing* was doing it! How?

"That doesn't matter," Clea said. "Go back to the main screen. Hm."

"There's no button that says *stop*." Deva checked her computer for any additional information but that was it. "What do we do?"

"Hit Relays," Clea replied. "Hurry."

Deva tapped the button and a map of the planet appeared with glowing points, presumably showing where the relays were. Another set of commands showed at the top, each representing the different facilities. When she tried one of them, it offered her several options for adjustment. She clicked one but a message appeared.

Must be in maintenance mode to proceed.
Deva heard Clea chuckle.

"That's it," Clea said. "The far left. Click that button."

It said *Administrator*. She tried it and various selections came up. *Reboot. Maintenance Mode. Standby*.

She tapped the second one but a message came up. *Active simulation in progress. Are you sure?*

"Yes! I'm way sure!" Deva tapped it again.

Negative survey results are guaranteed. Please confirm.

"C'mon!" Deva hit it again. "Yes, go go go!"

Soft shutdown initiated. Please wait.

"No!" Deva looked around frantically for another way to proceed.

"Slow down," Clea said. "I know your stressed down there but think about it for a moment. If it just shut down suddenly, it could cause some damage to the power core. And since you're standing on it, believe me, you want it to take the time it needs. I'm going to check the scans up here and see if it's working. Hang tight."

"Hold on, everyone!" Deva shouted. "We might have something!"

"What could it possibly be?" Lhar asked.

"A miracle," Deva replied, unable to stop smiling. "A real miracle."

***

Meagan zeroed in on another target, getting tone. She was about to hit the trigger when the thing literally vanished. "Oh, come on!" She shouted. "Are you flippin' kidding me right now?" Mick, did you see that?"

"Yeah, just happened to me too…" Ships began disappearing all around them, winking out of existence. Half the enemy fighter fleet was gone in an instant while the rest flashed out over the next several moments. They were suddenly alone out there with the four battleships and that was it.

Incredible, Meagan thought. *What happened?*

"Deploying bombs," Rudy called over the com. "All payloads."

That'll put an end to those battleships. Meagan looked around, regaining her wits. "Giant control, we need search and rescue out here to grab our disabled pilots. It appears that the fight is over."

"Acknowledged, return to the Behemoth for further instructions."

"You heard them," Meagan said to the rest of her wing. Confusion still clung heavily to her as they started flying back. "I hope someone knows what just happened because that will definitely go down as the strangest moment of my military career."

"Won't get an argument from me," Mick replied. "If the bombers successfully take out those ships, we might actually have won this one."

"Quite a miracle." Meagan shook her head. She ached to the bone and couldn't wait to get out of her cockpit. If half the pilots in her wing felt the same way, they all needed some serious downtime. Not just physically either. Witnessing what they had, seeing those enemies disappear...it would stick with them.

Lord knows we'll be asked for a psyche eval. Can't wait.

***

Adam tapped Gray's arm, drawing him from his own reports. "All enemy fighters are just...gone. They disappeared."

"Incredible." Gray looked up at the screen. The enemy battleships were still out there, still firing. "What about them? What's going on there?"

"Our bombers have just deployed their payloads," Adam replied, "they should make contact—" He fell silent as the ships disappeared...not exploded but were simply gone. Vanished like the fighters. "They're...we won!"

Leonard slumped in his chair in relief but Olly kept working hard. No one on the bridge seemed to have a celebration in them. Gray stood up, frowning at the screen. "I assume Clea will have an explanation for what we just witnessed. Definitely one of the more intense moments of my military career."

"Captain," Olly said, "I've got some bad news. Those ships disappeared before our bombs made contact."

"Okay?" Adam shrugged. "So what?"

"They're heading right for the planet."

"How many?" Gray asked.

"More than a dozen." Olly grunted, tapping at his terminal. "I've done some calculations. Whatever power core is down there *may* be destroyed by such an attack but...if so, it will detonate."

"And what's that mean for us?" Adam asked. "As in how bad will that be?"

"It's basically the most powerful power plant I've ever seen," Olly replied. "Means we'd have to jump out of here before it goes up or we'd all be dead. The people on the surface would be vaporized and any fighters out there wouldn't be able to escape the shockwave. It might be so big of an explosion, it could eventually mess with the gravitational motion of surrounding systems."

"Bad then," Gray said. "Have the pilots docked with the ship?"

Adam shook his head. "They're on the way though."

"Deploy them back. They have to take out those bombs before they make contact."

"Captain." Adam leaned forward, eyes wide. "That'll practically be suicide."

"We can't let this place be destroyed and if there are only twelve bombs, a full wing should be able to knock them out. They won't explode, correct?"

"They're set for contact detonation," Olly said. "So if they shoot them in the engine, they should be able to stop them."

"There you go." Gray gestured to Olly. "Adam, give the order. We need them to hurry. The next few moments will determine what happens to The Crystal Font and the people that I suspect saved us all down there. I'm not going to let them die simply for the convenience of flying off after all they did. Get to it."

***

Chapter 9

Alma and her wing wrapped up the last of the fighters on the planet surface and maintained a patrol pattern, prepared to support their people should they need cover to escape. It grated on her, listening to her colleagues in space battling overwhelming odds while she remained idle beneath them.

We should be up there right now. This is ridiculous.

Another squadron of enemies came from around the rise, but they were met with swift and decisive action. Alma's people went after them aggressively, leading with cannon fire. Though one managed to survive their initial attack, the way it spun away exposed its tail. Rahan put it down, dropping a continuous stream of fire until it erupted in flames.

Updates from within the structure also frustrated her. The soldiers dealt with a constant stream of ground forces, and though they seemed to be making good progress, she didn't envy them the constant action. *I'm glad to be behind the flight stick but I wish there was something we could do. We don't even know where they're all coming from!*

When they arrived at the control room, Alma wondered what it meant. Even if they brought out power, would they have the capacity to use it? Maybe the Behemoth could screen them. She listened to the battle, noting that they had taken down several of the enemy battleships. It seemed impossible, but perhaps they were witnessing a real miracle.

It might be nice for a change considering our normal poor luck.

"Alma, this is Varez." That particular tech officer always acted too familiar with other officers and she didn't like it. The man expressed precious little discipline, especially for a Zanthari. It was as if he didn't truly mean to join the military and would've been happier on board a merchant ship where rank didn't matter. "Do you read?"

"I'm here *Zanthari*." Alma emphasized his rank. "What's going on?"

Varez didn't seem phased. "The enemy fighters have vanished up here! They're simply gone!"

Alma frowned. *How? Why? I hope we have an explanation coming.* Instead of asking him any of her thoughts, she simply acknowledged the information. He likely had no better idea of how it happened than she did. Maybe Deva and Lhar figured something out. Either way, it meant her friends up there were no longer in danger. *That's a victory*.

"Is the shuttle incoming for pickup then?" Alma asked.

"Affirmative. It's on its way to collect the ground team." Varez paused. "Um...hold on."

I don't really have anywhere else to go! Alma felt grumpy from the entire situation but she hid it behind a deep breath. *What could be happening now? Can we really afford any more bad news?*

"I have some bad news," Varez said.

Of course you do! Alma gritted her teeth. "What is it?"

"Well...the battleships just winked out as well."

"How's that bad? I would imagine you guys didn't feel like brawling with them anymore."

"Yes, but...well...a lot of bombs were thrown at them."

"Is that how they *winked out*? Is this a new colloquialism I should be aware of?"

"They disappeared, Alma...but..." Varez cleared his throat. "They did so *before* the bombs hit. And now...the ordinance is heading for the planet."

Alma sat up straight, eyes wide. "How many?"

"A dozen."

"Are you joking? That's enough to sheer a continent if it hits in atmosphere!"

"Yes. So...that's where you come in."

"Let me guess, you want us to intercept?"

"You have to take out their engines before they wipe out everything in that region...and yes, I've done the math. They'll hit about six kilometers from the structure where our team is currently located."

"This is absolutely incredible." Alma sighed. "Rahan, Hilot, let's go. We have some work to do with some bombs." She filled them in on what was happening so they understood not only what they had to do but what was at stake as well. "You have to be careful what you shoot. Hitting the front would cause a lot of damage."

"I'm ready," Rahan said. "This sounds fun."

"Not the word I'd use," Hilot added, "but we'd better hurry."

Varez jumped in, "you'll be meeting two human pilots so please work together."

"We know what we're doing," Alma replied. "Just get us on their com net so we can talk and we'll take it from here. In fact, maintain silence unless you've got an urgent update. Hilot and Rahan, gun it and keep up. This is going to be one of the fastest departures we've ever made. I want to break atmo in less than a minute."

***

Meagan got the message from Revente just moments before she requested landing clearance. When he spoke to her, she instantly had a bad feeling and didn't hide her groan. The fact he called at all meant there was trouble. He never bothered with the basic tower control nonsense. *I'm not going to like this*.

"You're not going to like this," Revente started. Meagan rolled her eyes. "We've got a serious problem. Those bombs we fired at the enemy ships? They're still active...and they're on a direct course for the planet."

"Why do we care?" Meagan asked. "I mean, it's uninhabited, isn't it?"

"While that may be true, we're not in the habit of destroying worlds unnecessarily," Revente said. "Besides, our calculations put the impact points near enough to a kielan ground crew that none of them would survive. They need that power to get their ship out of here. We have to take the bombs down."

"Of course we do." Meagan closed her eyes and shook her head. "My wing can probably do it. What are there, twelve at most?"

"Yes, a dozen but you can't bring everyone. If there's a mistake...you know how it is. Too many cooks in the kitchen? The bombs are pretty tightly clustered so it wouldn't do to have a whole bunch of cannon fire out there."

"So how many do you want me to take?"

"Just you and Mick."

Meagan hesitated to reply and just shook her head again. "Are you insane? Two of us to take down twelve bombs?"

"You'll be met by three kielan pilots."

"Tell them to go home and I'll bring Panther wing with me. We'll each take one and that'll be eight down. The last four will be cake."

"The three kielans are closer and will likely get their first. I need you guys for hop up. Stop the engines and don't let them collide. They'll detonate on contact." Revente drew a deep breath. "You know I wouldn't ask this of you if I didn't think it was necessary."

"That doesn't make it better, just so you know." Meagan frowned and spun her ship around. "Come on, Mick. The rest of you land. We've got a quick chore to take care of. Revente, get me in touch with the kielan commander. I'd like to coordinate this so we don't blow each other up."

"Fair enough. I'm patching you through to their coms right now. Good luck and um…don't mess up. Too much at stake and all that."

"Yeah, I know. It's not like this is any different than the last ten missions I've been on. See you back on the ship." *I hope.*

***

Alma and her crew broke atmosphere far easier than she'd ever experienced on another planet, further emphasizing how strange the place proved to be. She didn't have time to think about it, focusing on the glowing bombs barely six-thousand kilometers away. They all popped up on her scanner, twelve of them, hurtling toward the planet at a rapid pace.

Estimated time to impact less than seven minutes.

"No pressure," she muttered. Switching to the com, she cleared her throat. "Human team, this is Vinthari Alma Il'Var. Do you read me?"

"Wing Commander Meagan Pointer here," came the reply. "We're on our way."

"We are focusing on those closest to the target...that being the planet." Alma cleared her throat. "As you're not here yet, you can pick up the rear. Is that agreeable?"

"Works for me," Meagan said. "Good luck."

Alma shoved the throttle forward, giving herself all the speed her fighter could produce. The others kept pace but spread out, preparing for the attack. Each of the missiles glowed from their engines, providing a beacon for what they were after. They moved around to get directly behind them before advancing further.

The action shouldn't have been a challenge. They were targets that wouldn't fire back after all but a mishap could be deadly. A wrong move meant detonating one of the warheads and at such a close proximity, it wouldn't go well for the smaller ships. For that reason, Alma reduced the power to her cannons and sent the message to her colleagues.

"We don't have to kick them to turn off those engines," Alma said. "Earth pilots, please note our tactic with our cannons. You need to vary your pulse blasts so you don't cause too much damage. I'll take the first shot. Hang back in case I make an instant hash of it."

Alma let the targeting computer search for a lock, closing the distance to speed up the process. As it began to beep, she knew she was close. The targeting reticle closed around the thruster then held a long tone. *I hope this works*. She tapped the trigger, sending a pair of blasts directly into her target.

The weaker blast struck the missile harder than expected. The ordinance spun until it faced up and away from the planet. The engine sparked, bursting a quick thrust which carried it a good distance away before fading out and drifting. Alma let out a breath she didn't even realize she was holding.

One down. "Turn down your weapons even more. That was a pretty hard hit and you saw what almost happened."

Hilot chuckled over the line. "You tend to be more forceful than is absolutely necessary."

Alma scowled, shaking her head. "Cut the chatter and focus."

She banked hard to the left and spun, coming in behind the next missile in the line. The estimated time to impact was five minutes. This didn't necessarily mean hitting the ground and causing damage. All they needed to do was break atmosphere and the mission would be a failure. Even knocking out their engines wouldn't save the world then.

We need to be a little more extreme I think. Eyeballing the shot, she fired three times, striking the next missile hard just above the engine near the guidance panel. Fire flared out of it and the entire back popped, sending shards of debris in every direction. The warhead spun to the left, no longer plunging for the surface.

Without hesitation, she continued down the line, taking shots. She missed three of them but caught the fourth, bringing it down safely. By the time she finished flying the line, she and the others took down six of the twelve. *This is not going fast enough*. The time to impact was only at three minutes.

"We're here," Meagan called out. "Weapons have been scaled and we're moving in to attack."

About time, Alma thought. "We'll circle around for an assist. At this point, we need to make attack runs to finish this off."

"I'm on it." Alma watched Meagan's ship fly past her, firing controlled bursts at the various missiles. She knocked two down in short order but the other four remained unscathed.

Hilot came after her, taking his first shot. He missed but in the worst possible way. His blast tapped the warhead. Alma was lining up for another attack run when she heard him gasp but she'd seen what he did. The bomb went off, exploding in a spectacular display. Hilot was far too close, his fighter's shields flared up then dropped.

As his craft was tossed backwards, he drifted a good hundred yards before his core went up and obliterated the entire ship. "No!" Alma called out. He didn't have the chance to eject but likely died the second the kinetic force struck his vessel. "Fall back! Everyone get out of there!"

The Earth fighters, Rahan and Alma all hit their afterburners and rushed away as the other three bombs went up. The explosion was nothing short of shocking and though they were already well away, the shockwave knocked Alma off course. She struggled with her controls, fighting to regain control and not run into one of her colleagues.

The others seemed to suffer the same but they were far enough apart to avoid a collision. Scanners went from a frantic beeping alarm to silence, stating they had reached a safe minimal distance. Alma turned her ship in a slow circle, looking back over what happened and where her squad mate died.

"Is everyone okay?" Thaina's voice came over the com. "How many detonated?"

"Four," Alma replied. "And no. Everyone is not okay. Zanthari Hilot Va'Doth was killed in action."

Thaina didn't respond immediately. "I see. It appears the threat's been eliminated...at quite the cost. Please return to The Crystal Font for a debriefing. Thaina out."

"I'm sorry," Meagan's voice came over her com. "I know what that's like and...all I can say is I'm sorry."

"I appreciate the sentiment," Alma replied. "Thank you for the assist. In coming here and with the bombs. Good bye." She banked back toward The Crystal Font and increased speed, trying to race off the anger she felt, the rage. Rahan gave her some space and didn't say anything but she knew he and Hilot were close friends.

I lost someone under my command but those two were inseparable. What a loss.

The fact they had the opportunity to get home felt bittersweet. Doing so without one of their own, without even a body to properly honor, made her heart heavy. *At least everyone else gets to return. You made a noble sacrifice, Hilot. Even if your bad aim got you killed. I'm sorry, my friend. You'll be missed.*

***

Deva turned in time to see Lhar and the others lower their weapons. The enemies in the hall had disappeared. Power readings returned to what they were when they first arrived in the system. Directing her attention to the massive monitor, a new set of words appeared. *Simulation complete.*

"It was not real!" Deva shook her head, dumbfounded. "None of it was real!"

"Yuris might disagree," Lhar said. "Those wounds were nasty."

A flash of light made Deva yelp before she could reply. A man appeared by the monitor, dark haired and dark eyed, wearing a white robe. He held up his hands as the others aimed weapons at him and he offered them all a smile. "Please, I do not mean you any harm. Also, I am not like the other projections. I am incorporeal."

"Wait!" Deva held up her hands to the others. "I'm on this." She turned to the man. "My name's Deva Thi'Noch. I'm with The Crystal Font, a starship from an alliance of many races. We're here in peace."

"Welcome! You may call me Bin. I do hope you enjoyed the game. I'm here to take your survey on how the facility performed."

"Are you kidding?" Lhar scoffed, advancing to stand beside Deva. "You nearly got us all killed!"

"We throttle the difficulty of the simulation based on performance," Bin replied. "As you struggled, we adjusted accordingly. Do you feel that we successfully met your expectations for a challenging and interesting event?"

Lhar walked away, reaching out to the ship. Deva watched him go for a moment but Bin repeated his question.

"Um…sure. Yes, you did."

"Excellent!" Bin smiled. "Were the details of your opponents accurate and expected?"

"Yeah, they seemed pretty real to me." Deva shrugged. "Bin, I appreciate that you need to ask us some questions but I really need some help. We have to have a power core to leave this system. It seems like you've got plenty to spare. How do I tap into it and bring enough back to my ship to go home?"

Bin blinked several times. "I am supposed to finish the survey but I can be flexible in my programming. We do have portable units for setting up simulations in any environment the planet can offer. We were required to shift orbit by nearly seven degrees to accommodate you physically so some of the realms are not prepared yet. Example, if you are interested in snow, we will not have enough for another full day."

"That's totally fine," Deva said, her eyes wide. "We just need a couple of those portable things if you don't mind."

A panel in the floor opened and two massive boxes slid out. "You may take these. How do you intend to use them?"

"Spark our crystal to go home?" Deva offered. "Do you know what that means?"

"Yes, we have evaluated your ship. You will need to fabricate an adapter. Please download the power core schematics from the middle terminal in order to make this work. Can we return to the survey now?"

"Um…later. When I return these, okay?"

Bin hesitated for a long moment. "That will be sufficient. Satisfaction is our aim. We cannot improve without feedback. Thank you for your participation in our game."

"Wait!" Deva held her hand out. "Who built this facility? When?"

"The Ela race built this facility at the height of their technological prowess. As they traveled the galaxy checking on various experiments, they realized they were going quite well and would one day need education and entertainment in equal measures. This facility was built with that in mind, tested by generations of Ela warriors and thrill seekers."

"Wait, the Ela?" Deva shook her head. "I've never heard of them."

"Ela extinction occurred nearly one hundred thousand years ago. Ten thousand years after this facility was constructed."

"Do you have historical records I can download? More information about the Ela?"

"Affirmative." Bin smiled. "Please access your computer and take the data you want from option number three."

"Thank you!" Deva complied, watching a percent meter quickly climb to one hundred. When she had the records, she turned back to Bin. "I appreciate your help and cooperation."

"I apologize for any inconvenience the game may have caused and look forward to the rest of your feedback. Farewell, kielan and good luck."

Bin vanished and Deva held her hand against her head, addressing Clea, "did you hear all that?"

"I did…" Clea hesitated. "I'm stunned. Good work getting the information and the power cores."

"I have to contact my own ship now for pickup," Deva replied. "Thanks for your help, Tathin An'Tufal. I appreciate it!"

"I look forward to talking to you more about all of this while we get your ship ready to go," Clea replied. "See you soon."

Deva turned to the others and directed them toward the massive boxes. "We have what we came for. Let's get up there and make them work, huh?"

"About time we get out of here," Trias said. "I took one to the arm at the end of that fight. Armor's dented. It hurts like a rellan."

"Colorful," Lhar muttered. "Shuttle's on the way. Let's find out how heavy these things are and get back to civilized space. It's safe to say I'm pretty much done with games for the foreseeable future…possibly forever."

***

Kale took in the various reports with a mixture of feelings but relief trumped them all. He felt terrible for the pilot, Hilot. Losing anyone was frustrating. The injured soldier, Yuris, would recover and have little scarring somehow. The physicians truly were artisans to pull that one off considering how badly the armor had melted over him.

But they received the power core and would return with a major archaeological find. Deva was thrilled beyond belief and requested time to speak with Clea An'Tufal in person. He granted it during the time they would be swapping out the crystal. She would not be needed for that process.

He returned to his quarters and contacted Captain Atwell on the Behemoth, asking for a brief, private conversation. The other commander agreed and a moment later, they were face to face, at least over a screen.

"Seems like a lifetime ago when I told you I'd cover your escape," Kale said. "Thank you for coming for us."

"It was the least we could do after the research facility," Gray replied. "But based on the information you shared, it sounds like you might've made it without us."

"Maybe...but there's no guarantee." Kale shrugged. "In any event, as soon as we spark the crystal, we can all get out of here. I'll owe you a meal. Perhaps on the home world if you're coming back with us."

"We are," Gray said. "There's something I should tell you about our arrival. We didn't know you'd survived to be honest. Your message was garbled and missing the coordinates. Alliance intelligence gave us the task of finding you. They thought we'd be motivated and were right but their reasons weren't entirely altruistic."

"I see." Kale frowned. "Are they expecting something in return?"

Gray nodded. "They're going to recruit you."

Kale smirked, turning away.
"Interesting...but not unexpected. A jump mishap and a couple of close calls make us eligible and qualified for intelligence work. I'm assuming this is not the type of 'opportunity' you say 'no' to, right?"

"We haven't been able to," Gray said. "My government leant us out but it hasn't been all bad. We got to come here and we stopped a civil war...fought terrorists. We're building up to the final battle with the Devarans too."

Kale raised his brow. "I feel that I've missed a lot."

"You have, my friend." Gray leaned back in his chair. "Let me tell you about some of it. I hope you've got something to drink. This is going to take a while."

Epilogue

Siva was on her way into the base when she received a text communication from The Behemoth on her private com. She paused in an awning, allowing her bodyguards to take up positions on either side. The message appeared, decrypting in real time. The fact they adhered to security protocols gave her confidence in the offer she made before they left.

Siva,The Crystal Font is secure and we'll be coming home in roughly ten shifts. We'll need medical attention for some of these folks and I'm thinking a few of them will want leave. I've attached a full report of the situation but I request that you leverage a quarantine to this sector of space. It is not safe.

Please let me know if you have any questions. Signed, Clea An'Tufal.

"Good girl, An'Tufal," Siva muttered. "Excellent work. One more ship for the cause."

As she boarded the elevator, Siva felt particularly pleased. Having a second military vessel at her disposal meant so much to her operations. Now that they were on the verge of a full scale attack, she needed people to take care of the oblique threats, the dangers that weren't quite so overt.

Arriving at her station, she acknowledged Clea's remarks and made the requested arrangements. Then she opened up her operations board and started planning exactly what to do with The Crystal Font and the Behemoth in the coming weeks leading up to the big fight. Considering their successes, they both might need some down time but it would have to be quick.

We have a war to win, after all. Several, in fact. And I don't intend to let a single one of these threats go by without opposition. I hope you're ready for a real challenge, Kale Ru'Xin. Because I'm about to give you one.

***

Trellan set his ship down in a pirate port he'd been to on several occasions, heading immediately for the port master. The portly man leaned against a wall, dozing. A tap to the side of the head made the poor bastard scream and he nearly collapsed, glaring with such rage, it was good looks couldn't kill.

"Glad you're so aware," Trellan muttered. "I feel like my stuff is safe with you watching it."

"Shove off," the port master said. "I don't have to take your guff. What do you want?"

"I need to stay here for a while and I've got goods to trade. Who do I see about the exchange?"

"Go to the market!" The portly fellow moved over to a chair and plunked himself down in it. "I don't have time for you."

"Okay then." Trellan departed and headed deeper into the port, looking around for where they might take his goods. He needed money for weapons, a change of clothes and sadly, he had to sell the stuff the civilians had on board. *All for the cause. It's nothing personal. Wow, my conscious is really getting to me this time*.

He'd stolen plenty in his time undercover but for whatever reason, this last theft really bothered him. Those people were the exact type he was sworn to protect from Orion's Light and others. Instead, he at the very least complicated their lives and at the worst ruined them. *I've become what I'm hunting*.

A couple hours later, he'd sold the goods and changed into something more casual. Fully armed again, he felt more himself and took up at a hotel for a bath and some downtime. Men and women shoved into the bar and he found himself amongst them that evening, hoping for a meal and some relaxation.

Then a geran started boasting about his combat prowess and someone promised to shut him up. Blows were thrown. Trellan found himself in the tick of a full on barroom brawl. After knocking out a freighter pilot and one of his crewman, he realized he was the only person in the place that was alone.

Slipping outside, he decided to take a walk, hurrying down the street to nurse a blow to his chin he didn't remember taking. *This life is something else. Chaotic...and predictable. I can't wait for the assignment to be over. No one can live like this for long. Not without losing their minds...or worse*.

"Hey," a voice called out, drawing his attention from across the street. "You looking for work? Saw what you did back there and you can really handle yourself."

Will it always start like this?

"Depends on the job," Trellan said. "I'm looking for a cause...not just some easy money."

"Then, brother, do I have something for you. I can't talk about my employers but believe me, they're all about the cause."

"Then let's talk." Trellan joined him and gestured down the street. "Maybe over a drink? I've had a long day."

Made in United States
Orlando, FL
19 June 2022

18955435R00157